Fort Destiny

Fort Destiny

By
SAMUEL O. SISCO
and
BERT M. SISCO

A MAN'S FORT IS HIS CONSCIENCE,
HE ALONE CAN MAKE A HELL OF IT!

AVALON BOOKS

THOMAS BOUREGY AND COMPANY, INC.

22 EAST 60TH STREET · NEW YORK 10022

PUBLISHED SIMULTANEOUSLY IN THE DOMINION OF CANADA
BY THE RYERSON PRESS, TORONTO

PRINTED IN THE UNITED STATES OF AMERICA
BY THE COLONIAL PRESS INC., CLINTON, MASSACHUSETTS

DEDICATION

To Our

"Darlin' Mama" for her creative teachings.

And for Buzzy and Gene, brothers both . . .
But different as the Blue and the Gray!

Samuel O. Sisco
Bert M. Sisco

SPECIAL NOTE

This book is a work of fiction, taking place in 1865; but then again it is war fiction. Are peoples' emotions fiction? The vehicle of its birth was the bloodiest Civil War the world had known—a war that resulted from the actions of headstrong men unable to agree why they fought.

They are nearly all gone now . . . the hundreds of thousands of the armies, the millions waiting at home. Their task is done, the record written, their legacy is upon us.

We cannot blind ourselves to those four tragic years of bloodletting; the Federal dead were counted at 360,222 and the Federal wounded at 275,175. The Confederate dead were put at 258,000, and no one could say how many had been wounded. Between 1861 and 1865 there were close to two million soldiers who fought for Mr. Lincoln. How many served under arms for the Confederacy remains unknown. A reasonable estimate is between 600,000 and 700,000.

The world watched this war; it had lessons for people everywhere. It was terrible, and yet grand; fearful, and yet inspiring; tragic, and yet satisfying. And when the guns were stilled, the dead were

buried, and when succeeding springs laid gentle
cloaks over the scars of the battlefields, the indisputable
decision . . . the Thirteenth Amendment
. . . could not be ignored. In the end, it justified a
time-honored faith . . . "that this nation, under
God, shall have a new birth of freedom." And with it
came responsibilities still unmet.

War is something that seeps down into deep crevices
of the human soul and, despite great effort, can
never be routed out. The deeds are history; what use
we make of them is our trust. No one person, no one
leader, no one writer, will use them, or should use
them, the same way as another. There was room for
dispute then; let it always be so.

The Civil War . . . all life . . . is surely more
than just the bareness of events, the moving, the
death, of men on the chessboard by historians. . . .
Here then is a glimpse into the personal, the minor
acts, the trifles that make up all life, including war. It
is the ancient epic brought to our own day, near
enough to capture a sense of danger, the immediacy
of determining wrong from right and the intimacy of
it.

War, be it fought with guns or within minds, is a
horrible, unnecessary evil in all its aspects. Why,
then, do we have so much of it? Why, then, are songs
written about it; why do poets chant, historians make
recountings, and storytellers weave their themes?
Few souls condone it, least of all the man behind the
gun. But within the holocaust of times is discovered
the human spirit with a basic soundness, a mysterious

impulse that causes man to realize what is within his own self.

Fort Destiny will not solve any questions of the Civil War, nor of one man. It will not clear up the perplexing issues of that day, or of this. Those tasks are left for the historian and, we hope, the politician. But here is a part of your legacy, your Civil War—a time and a place when men searched for medicines to counteract fear, gloried in the clamor for fame, lost their perspective in faith, and forgot the power of love.

Here then, is a Civil War. Live it as you will . . . with each man to his own fort.

Healdsburg, California
June 1, 1964

Samuel O. Sisco
Bert M. Sisco

CHAPTER ONE

Before the spring of 1861 many Americans had never seen a soldier in uniform; now armed men were everywhere. North and South, state militia, dazzled by the flashy troops of Napoleon III, dressed like the Zouaves of Algeria in baggy red trousers, white or yellow gaiters, short blue embroidered jackets and red fezzes with their long blue tassels. The Garibaldi Guards, New York's Thirty-ninth Infantry, adopted the dress of Italian Bersaglieri, straight up to the plumed hat; the Seventy-ninth New Yorkers were Highlanders in colorful Scottish sporrans and kilts. The Second Wisconsin were smartly uniformed in gray—much to their sorrow, when Union troops fired on them in battle. Even Confederate generals like Joe Johnston, Beauregard and Jackson appeared quite often in the old blue uniforms of their Regular Army days.

On April 23, 1861, Secretary of War Cameron specified as the regulation Union uniform a dark-blue flannel sack coat, light-blue kersey trousers, flannel shirt, forage cap, bootees and stockings; but Cameron issued an empty order until combat taught the ninety-day boys that peacock feathers were not the

most intelligent garb where bullets whizzed. About
the same time, the Confederate gray became official;
yet many Southern regiments clung to the smart blue
uniforms in which they had already invested.

With rollicking bands playing, the boys gathered
at county seats, where they were usually herded in
pairs into a room. Here a doctor yelled "Strip!"
looked them over like a team of horses up for sale,
and told them to sign a paper.

And so, within a few minutes, the boys lost their
status as civilians. Mothers, wives, and sweethearts
wept and embraced them. Fathers shook hands, and
little brothers gazed in envy. Then by rail, steamer
and on foot, Yank and Reb journeyed to their state
capitals.

The tiredness, both mental and physical, experienced in war is so great that sleep cannot lift it. The
endless tired feeling builds up slowly inside, then so-
lidifies like old age. And the queer sensation taking
over the body is that of instinctive wisdom—a feeling
never felt before. But with the sudden wisdom comes
less and less strength to appreciate it, even to realize
it's there.

The tiredness, the wisdom, had no affect on Lieutenant Walker Decklin, squatting on the sod floor of
the relay station, his wrists handcuffed behind his
back. Six Apaches, remaining of yesterday's raiding
band of eleven, kept running their ponies around the
building, shouting, laughing at the burned stagecoach and making wild gestures with their stolen
rifles—this morning, not firing them, but threatening.

That shrewd playing on a man's nerves was the thing
that gave the lieutenant his first feeling: Fear . . .

That fearful anguish nailed him to the spot; but
any man who got this close to a band of Apache warri-
ors without being afraid was a fool. And any man
who got himself in the witless predicament of being
handcuffed in the presence of the Apache, and not
being able to convince his captors to unlock the
chains—in Lieutenant Walker Decklin's book of sur-
vival, he had removed all doubt as to his stupidity.

His heart was thudding heavily as he glanced up at
his commanding officer, Major Mitchel of Missouri's
31st Dragoons, who knelt by the arrow-smashed window, fidgeting about, trying to find a comfortable position, his carbine resting on the jagged sill. Beside
Mitchel was his young aide, Trooper Roark, a rifle
stock slammed up against his right shoulder, the barrel of it pocked alongside the major's; the aide sat
still, like a meditating Buddha. What gave Trooper
Roark distinction was the metal box, no larger than a
woman's small traveling sewing kit, chained and se-
curely locked to his left wrist. The civilian and the
woman at the far side of the room couldn't keep their
eyes from it.

Noticing the quietness of his aide, Mitchel ceased
his shifting about on his knees. There seemed to be
tranquillity in his muscles, but there was a hunger in
his eyes the way they darted and followed the war-
riors' every threatening rifle and bow rise, his tensed
trigger finger ready to touch off the hair thread of his
own fright.

Deep in the back of Lieutenant Decklin's mind he nurtured the thought that Mitchel would free his hands before the Apaches made their final rush. But when Major Mitchel glanced over his shoulder, and Decklin looked into the major's deep-set eyes, Decklin couldn't find a single scrap of hope.

The second feeling came swiftly on the heels of the lieutenant's fear. It was a fierce and terrible sensation, but a man's contact with his conscience is always fierce and terrible, like the flashing red lantern at the train crossing that doesn't keep the man from trying to beat the train. The lieutenant suppressed a tiny smile, knowing of no other witness so damning, no accuser so powerful as a man's conscience. He clenched his fists behind his back, straining against the metal chains on his wrists. What he had done, he'd do all over again. His lips thinned; ever since he could remember, he had lived with that flashing red lantern swinging before him. . . .

Walker Decklin's rule was: If you think you're right, go ahead and do it! A man just has to be in the right place at the right time, and he has it made.

The lieutenant smiled openly now; he *had* been in the right place at the right time, but being there backfired. His fists clenched again, the chain biting harder into his wrists.

In his discomfort he shifted his shoulders against the wall and looked out through the broken window-pane. The early sun struck its brightness on the metal buttons on his blue jacket and flashed along the metallic telegraph wire strung out along the vast flat plains. He cursed that shiny wire for being out of order now, and cursed it for being in order three days ago, hastening his capture.

The Apaches began kicking up the pace of their ponies, feinting now at the west wall of the relay station where the civilian huddled on the floor of the two-room cabin, the woman beside him tightly clutching his arm.

The civilian said, "They'll attack again, won't they?" The edge of cowardice seemed forced in his voice, as if it didn't rightly belong there. The revolver at his hip held the sheen of hard use and tender care; but the weapon had remained holstered all through yesterday's siege.

Lieutenant Decklin turned a baleful glance on the man. "Scares you? You got a gun. Use it."

Temper rushed dark and full-blown through the major's hard face, and his oath broke through the hush that had quickly bridged between the lieutenant and the civilian. "Shut your mouth, Lieutenant Decklin. I told you before I don't want to hear one peep outa you!"

He stood and spun on the civilian. "You were told this run was to have no passengers. You talked me into letting you and your woman come with us, so *use* your gun!" His eyes became tiny steel rings around the dead black of the pupils. "I'll not tell you again!"

The major did not like the civilian's looks. The

man was dressed in the fashion of a rich plantation owner—handsome, in an obvious fashion—but there was something sinister about the way he smiled.

The civilian shrugged his wide shoulders, gave the major a widening grin and glanced over at the lieutenant and said, "I don't believe in violence."

"The devil with your belief," snapped the major.

"Sir," interrupted Trooper Roark, "I think they're going to charge us."

The major quickly turned back to the window.

"Violence doesn't bother me," said Lieutenant Decklin, twisting sideways and showing his cuffed wrists. For the fifth time since the Apaches began their assault, he said, "Major . . . unlock these."

Without taking his gaze off the Indians, the major laughed. "Think I'm crazy? I know you're aching to get your hands on that box."

"Sir, I told you before, I don't care what he's carryin'. I'm only interested in gettin' to Fort Ward . . . *alive!*"

Still not turning to look at his prisoner, the major mumbled, "What for? To stand before a firing squad?"

Fear of the Apaches taking him alive, with his hands chained, lashed at him like a whip. He pulled himself to his feet and stood towering above the major's kneeling form. He drew up his boot, and smashed the sole of it hard against the major's shoulder, slamming him lengthwise to the ground. "My crime does not permit you, *sir*, to judge me

. . . or to let the Apache get me like this. Damn you. *sir,* you unlock these cuffs!"

Major Mitchel swung his rifle around, leveling the barrel at Decklin's stomach. "Cuffed or uncuffed, Lieutenant," he gritted, getting an elbow up under him and quickly pulling his back against the wall, "you're a doomed man. Sit down or I'll shoot you down!"

Lieutenant Decklin watched him stonily for a moment, then said, "Since you've set yourself up as judge and jury, go ahead and shoot!"

A gunshot rang out like an ominous voice.

The surprise of it was like having the floor jerked out from beneath the lieutenant's feet. But he did not fall; nor did he feel the slam of the bullet striking his body. He turned toward the sound and saw Trooper Roark's smoking rifle aimed out the window, just as the shotgun guard burst from the small rear room that housed the telegraph equipment. The man yelled, "Here they come! Did you drop one, Trooper?"

Roark shook his head. "Missed."

Major Mitchel spun his bottom on the floor and quickly pulled himself up to the sill, grabbing an overturned wooden packing crate and sitting on it, forcing his rifle barrel into firing position, in that one explosion of movement.

"Wait until they get closer," said Mitchel to Roark. "Our ammunition is near gone." Then throwing Lieutenant Decklin a backward glance, he growled, "If we get out of this, I doubt very much if you'll see Fort Ward . . . I'll personally see to it that you don't!"

"That a threat, *sir?*"

Mitchel's fleeting glance turned now into a hard stare. "No, Lieutenant. That's a promise!"

The wiry shotgun guard, dressed in grease-soiled buckskins, yelled again as he leaped for the door, pulling it slightly ajar to get his carbine out. "Turn the prisoner loose! We'll need every gun!"

The major ignored the man, even when the paunchy coach driver staggered from the back room, stepping over the dead station attendant, and said, "Major, you're a regulation-totin' fool!" He put a hand to the scarlet-blotched rag tied about his head and weaved his way to the main room's second window. He called over his shoulder to Decklin, "Lieutenant, I don't like your major. Before this is over, I just might shoot him for you."

"You can always try." Mitchel nodded grimly. Then he said to the civilian, "Do I have to tell you not to let the Apaches capture her?" He nodded at the woman. "You can do *that,* can't you?"

The civilian stood up, and from across the room pointed his finger towards Mitchel's window. "Wait," he said. "I don't think they'll attack again. Don't shoot . . ."

Lieutenant Walker Decklin turned to face the civilian; the angered fury of knowing the man fired old remembrances. "You know a lot for a coward!"

The civilian turned his back on him, helped the

woman to her feet, then went to the window. "See—" He pointed a white-gloved hand. "They're just going to make a run to drag off their dead."

The civilian was correct. The Apaches came in on a fast gallop, picked up their dead, tossed the bodies across their bare knees, and took off across the plains, waving guns and bows in the air. Their yelling screeches came back in hollow echoes.

"My bet is, they've gone for help," muttered Lieutenant Decklin. Standing beside the civilian, he matched the man's six-foot-four tallness, inch for inch.

"He's right," said the stage driver. "If we don't get outa here, this station is gonna be our coffins. Let's travel while we're able."

Mitchel took a deep breath. "They set fire to the stage, chased off all the stock, didn't they? How do we get out? Fly?"

"I managed to corral three teams," said the driver. "The coach is a little singed but in runnin' order. We'd better fan a fire under *us* though. Can't wait for Army regulations . . ."

"Sounds intelligent," mumbled Mitchel. He turned to the lieutenant and said, "I have a notion to leave you here."

"Do it," grinned Decklin. "But I doubt it. You have too many witnesses."

Major Mitchel's jaw line gave a visible clamp. Without further word, he motioned the lieutenant toward the rear door.

Suddenly the tick-ticking of the telegraph in the

back room began. They stopped, momentarily stunned.

Mitchel looked down at the dead station attendant. "It's a wonder the Apache didn't cut the wire before it was repaired. Trooper Roark, you can read Morse code? Get to it!"

"Yes, sir."

"Ask for help. Tell whoever is on the wire that we have to leave and say where we're headed."

With the metal case clutched in his hand, the small chain about it and his wrist dangling loosely, Roark ran to the back room and sat at the small table.

Mitchel herded the lieutenant after Roark, and the civilian and the woman crowded in after them.

The clicking of the key was running wild as a nervous child banging on tin plates. Suddenly the sound stopped on a high pitch. Roark looked up, face grim and blank all at one. "No need to wonder why it hasn't been cut, sir," he said. "It just was."

"Could you make out anything?"

"Something about that Confederate Colonel Viking being captured seven days ago at Camp Mac-Millan."

"Good. I'd like to be there when they stand him before a firing squad."

Roark stood. "That's not all, sir. Colonel Viking escaped four days ago and killed three guards. Seems he knows about this, sir." He rattled the metal case at his wrist.

"Anything about the Apaches?"

"Something about Spotted Bear's renegade

Apaches being farther north . . . then it went
dead."

"Farther north, my foot," grumbled the major.
"We just had a go with them, and we aren't *north*
yet."

"Which way *are* we going?" asked the woman, still
clinging onto the civilian's arm.

Mitchell looked at her. A spark of pity came into
his face. "We must reach Fort Ward. There's only
one way to take, Miss. North."

"Ready," called the stage driver, looking in the
back door. "The coach ain't the height of fashion.
Fire-gutted it sure is, but got usable wheels under it.
Let's move out." He laughed a shrill, high laugh, like
the crow of a cock. "By glory, we'll be ridin' Hell on
wheels."

Morning sun, raw as the grazing Texas plains and
relay station it blistered, slapped across Lieutenant
Walker Decklin's shoulders as he stooped uncomfor-
tably to get into the burnt stagecoach. Major Mitchel
and Trooper Roark were tight at his heels. The civilian and woman had already found their seats.

Wrists handcuffed behind his back made the lieutenant's entrance clumsy; he fell against the civilian's
knee. The man quickly offered him a hand.

"Keep your filthy hands off me, Hib," said Decklin.

"Knock it off, Walk, or you'll spoil it," whispered
the civilian. "Julie and I'll get you outa this mess.
You can bet on that. I promise you."

"You can take your promises straight to blazes."

"Ah, Walk," muttered the man.

"I told you before. Don't go out of your way to do me any favors."

"Still sore about Susan." The civilian moved both his gloved hands in an upward gesture. "Walk, you can have it your way—but you won't be able to live with it. Before Susan died, she wanted us to remain friends." He dropped his hands and reached one out to pull the lieutenant in. "Let's keep it that way."

Lieutenant Walker Decklin jerked his shoulders from the hand, letting his body fall in the seat across from the man and woman. His voice was hardly above a hoarse whisper: "You killed her, Hib, sure as if you put a gun to her head."

The civilian's long frame tightened as if a Bowie knife had been shoved in his ribs. "In other words, if Susan would have married *you,* she'd still be alive, alive to see you like this? Nothin' but a common thief . . . ."

"A thief because of a responsibility you've forgotten." Decklin's voice raised. "But I see loss of Susan hasn't slowed you down, Hib." He looked over at the woman. "Still playin' for high stakes, Julie?" He slowly shook his head from side to side. "You both really here to help me—or does Roark's metal box have something to do with your sudden appearance?"

"That's enough," snapped the civilian. Bending forward, his white-gloved hand streaked out and connected squarely across the lieutenant's mouth.

The lieutenant stiffened.

"Hib, don't," said the woman softly, pulling on the man's arm. "If Walk wants to, he could ruin everything. All he has to do is tell the major he knows us . . ."

The civilian patted her hand. "He won't ruin his only chance of escaping, my dear. Walk will let me do this one favor for him. I owe it to him."

Lieutenant Decklin's voice rose higher than he intended. "Conscience trouble? Never thought *you* had one."

Major Mitchel's bulk shoved into the coach. "Lieutenant," he growled, "you sure took your time getting in!" He sat beside Decklin. Immediately he sensed the steel tautness of the lieutenant's frame; noticed the manner in which he stared across at the civilian; noticed the finger marks starting to crimson on the lower part of his face. "You know this man?" he asked, nodding at the civilian.

Decklin's face looked hard as old rawhide. "What man?"

"Lieutenant," gritted the major, "your court-martial can only dispose of your crimes and insubordination once. But before you're shot, you answer my questions with an answer—not another question. *Do you know him?*"

Decklin shook his head.

Major Mitchel scrutinized the civilian. The man well might be a spying Confederate glory-hunter—especially one for Colonel Viking. Thoughts exploded like a myriad of tiny spears in his brain. No one had ever gotten a good look at Colonel Viking, and traveling on a mission such as Mitchel was, carrying a gold map worth more than a million dollars to the Union . . .

"Name's Kinsman—Hib Kinsman from New Orleans." The civilian pulled off his glove and extended his hand. "This rogue," he nodded at Decklin, "insulted Miss Booth here. Sorry if I had to slap him down."

The major took the offered hand, still finding caution in its weak-pressured fingers.

"Sorry if I've been a little gruff," said the major. "But you understand there were to be no passengers on this run."

Julie Booth, smoothing down her wrinkled green broadcloth skirts, entwined her arm in Hib Kinsman's and looked across at Decklin. "We're going to be married when we reach Springfield, Missouri." She quickly looked over at the major, fearing he would detect the hidden sharpness of her words. "That's why we wanted on this stage so bad. It was the only one going north."

The major grumbled his best wishes and helped Roark into the coach, who handed in a brown leather case. The aide had the major's cape tossed over his left arm, concealing the metal box chained to his wrist.

Shoving the leather satchel between the coach's burnt wood side and Decklin, the major said, "Don't see what use you'll have for this."

Sunlight shone on the satchel and the gold-plated tag along the top, housing the engraved lettering:

Lieutenant Walker Decklin D.V.M. Union Army, 31st Dragoons.

Smiling with forced coyness, the woman said, "Why he's a veterinarian. How quaint."

Decklin said, "I've met better horses than some men."

"Knock it off, Lieutenant," snapped Major Mitchel. Then, squinting his eyes against the sun, he leaned across Decklin and called up to the driver: "Let's move out. We've got a lot of miles to cover to reach Fort Ward by tomorrow."

The coach jolted forward at the driver's cry and snap of the whip above the horses' rumps.

CHAPTER TWO

Ten miles out, Decklin saw the telltale smoke—a thin lifting pennant, puffing gray against the mottled brass-bright desert. Because it came from a mesa top, and not the valley leading into Oklahoma's Fort Ward, it read to him and also to Spotted Bear's renegade Apache lookouts on the mountains ahead, "White men coming!"

Clatter of the teams hoofs striking rocks ushered the arrival of the stagecoach into Indian territory like a column of cavalry. Walker Decklin's face showed weariness, but his eyes were bright with an interest and knowledge that hadn't died since his capture three days ago at Clear Fork, Texas. That was when Hib Kinsman and Julie Booth got on the coach. No matter what he thought of Hib Kinsman, Hib would help him escape.

The shimmering noonday heat had bleached the sky to a whitish, skim-milk blue. Decklin searched for movement out on the plains, out across the dusty desert floor, squinting at the looming mountains. A bobcat was briefly outlined as he walked disdainfully from rock to rock; later a coyote, alarmed by the clattering noise of the coach, slunk quickly into a dry arroyo. Then for no apparent reason the coyote took to running across the flat, as if someone had tied a bucket of rocks to its tail.

Visibly backtracking the coyote's action, the lieutenant sucked in his breath with a deep gasp. There at the far end of the arroyo, silhouetted on the cutbank, and partly hidden from view by scrub oak, sat two Confederates on snappy spotted Appaloosa horses and three horse-backed Apaches—friendly as a flock of crows holding a big caw-cuss in a corn patch. One bare-chested Indian pointed at the coach and raised his bow.

Decklin pulled his head from the window of the swaying conveyance, turned to Major Mitchel. "Unlock these," he said. There was no pleading in the tone as he rolled his shoulders and twisted sideways to show steel cuffs that had bit crimson ruts into his wrists.

Julie Booth put a hand to her throat. Hib Kinsman patted her arm with his spotless white-gloved hand, restraining her.

Again Lieutenant Decklin spoke. "Major, give me a chance to defend myself."

"Settle down. We've seen the Apaches," said the major, turning a baleful glance on his prisoner. "If worse comes to worst, I'll give you the key. Until then, no!"

Anger came high in Decklin's voice. "If it means anything, *sir,* Confederates are riding with the Apaches. It could well be Colonel Viking."

"Hogwash! Even this Colonel Viking wouldn't stoop that low."

"If Viking wants something bad enough, he'll stoop lower."

"Apaches or Confederates or Colonel Viking, you wear the bracelets until I *say* they come off."

Decklin thought about pressing the conversation further; instead, he matched the major's stare with eyes that seemed to strip bare Mitchel's innermost thoughts. "If I don't reach Fort Ward alive, I swear I'll come back from hell and kill you . . . *sir!*"

"That will be your privilege, Lieutenant."

Lieutenant Walker Decklin straightened in his seat, and found Hib Kinsman watching his every move. It had been nearly five years since he'd looked into Hib's eyes as he was doing now. Still, he found them to be savage and lonely as he remembered them. Decklin found himself wondering why the man hadn't used a gun on the Apaches. Never before had he known Hib to back down from a fight; had the war turned him into a coward, or was he pretending? Decklin's brow wrinkled in wonderment and Hib caught the trace of the frown. Quickly Hib Kinsman gave his head a slight shake and winked slyly.

Immediately Decklin went back to glaring at the silent-talking smoke puffs on the flat-topped hill, and his mind became occupied with the woman sitting beside Hib Kinsman—Julie Booth, who would throw water on a drowning man if it would better her position in society. Hib and Julie were suited for each other as much as any two cunning, lying humans could ever be. The two people he'd least expect help from, proved by their presence his only friends.

Decklin braced his shoulders against the worn, fire-singed seat back, against the coach's jolting rattle, trying to ease his chained wrists behind him to a more comfortable position, and not succeeding. He went back to watching the curling smoke plume.

Suddenly the smoke completely vanished.

With his searching eyes on the level plains, his mind miles away, he felt the pressure of his conscience that had gotten him in this predicament. His eyes were slitted, holding in the force of his thoughts. Arriving at Fort Ward would satisfy his conscience, if what he had done was fully justified.

Anxious to know how far it was to the fort, he pushed his head out of the window and called up to the shotgun guard, "How long before we reach Fort Ward?"

The buckskin-clad man turned his head downward and let fly a brown liquid stream of tobacco juice.

"Fifteen miles, give or take one. We've been in Oklahoma the past hour," he called out above the pound of the hoofs. "We'll make Fort Ward in one piece," he added, "if we beat them there Injuns off yonder. You folks got anything on your conscience, now by glory is the time to get it off your chests!"

Decklin had to pull his head quickly inside to miss the splatter of tobacco juice as it hit the side of the coach. Instantly the man's words began Decklin's brain cogs to turning, and he wondered how much a man really let his conscience rule him.

Cowardice asks: Is it safe? Vanity asks: Is it proper? But conscience asks: Is it right? Walker Decklin knew there were times when a man needed to back himself off in a corner to evalute his own measure— to find out how much trouble a man's conscience gave him. He'd known men who'd said they had none. Hib Kinsman was one. And he wondered now, how true their words were.

Ever since he was a kid in short pants, doing the wrong thing always provoked him. And for seventeen of his thirty years, the weight of a kid's error hovered over him like a black cat's overcoat. It never seemed to bother Hib Kinsman, no matter how wrong they both were, when Joel Decklin had been cut down from their target practicing and left a cripple.

But what he had done two months ago, to help remedy a kid's mistake—he had no feeling that it *was* wrong. To Walker Decklin's way of thinking, there are things a man has to do, even if it looks wrong.

He rehashed his actions as they would be written on the official report: Desertion. Horse theft. Armed robbery of government property and payroll. No matter how he looked at the future, it spelled out court-martial and death. The odds were stacked against him.

One thing was clear to him now: he hadn't escaped the punishment he deserved for past actions; he had only delayed its coming.

Julie Booth, straightening her skirts again, saw the concern on Decklin's face. She faked a cough, attracted his attention and offered him a faint smile. A frown creased her features as she noticed the awkward way he was forced to hold his arms behind him.

She turned all her fury on the major and his aide, who had not once shifted the position of his clutched cape since entering the coach.

"What kind of men are you?" she snapped. "You know the Apaches are watching us. How can you be so inhuman as to keep your prisoner handcuffed? I demand you free him!"

Decklin was hard put for a moment to hide the smile that threatened to turn his lips. This was it, he thought. Nothing like a woman's wrath to unravel a man's watchfulness.

"I'm afraid, Miss," began the major, "there's more at stake, here, than the uncomfortableness of a prisoner."

Those words struck a chord in Decklin's mind. Ever since Clear Fork he had wondered why the major would track down a common thief and deserter. Decklin began feeling like a fifth ace in a poker deck. Was the metal case chained to Roark's wrist the *real* reason Julie and Hib were here?

The brilliant hues of the setting sun dyed the thin clouds gold and rose, then slowly faded to purple and gray. Walker Decklin continued to stare out at the darkening landscape, absorbed and entranced by the way it could hide the largest rock formations.

The coach's jolting increased, for here the road became more rocky and rougher. Decklin braced himself more firmly and heard Julie utter a low, protesting groan as the wheels rammed into a boulder that nearly overturned the coach.

The sudden jerk threw Major Mitchel against Decklin the same instant a shrill cry made the lieutenant lift his eyes to the slope above. He saw dust boiling up from the hoofs of a dozen plunging Apache ponies, the Indians clinging like cockleburrs to the backs of those sliding horses.

"Here come your Apaches," mumbled Decklin.

"Any Confederates?" quickly asked Mitchel.

"Can't see any."

Mitchel let an I-told-you-so look smirk on his face. Then the Indians' cries lifted like shrill coyote barks in the quiet, hot air. Mitchel and Roark snapped around. The girl grew restless, the fear of the unknown wrinkling her forehead. Hib Kinsman seemed unconcerned, sitting straight-backed against the seat, his hands neatly folded in his lap; but his face was settling into a solemn cast.

The shotgun of the guard up on the box roared once . . . twice. The driver's long whip cracked savagely. The teams lunged their shoulders against collars and broke into a hard gallop.

It all happened so fast that by the time Decklin turned to look across at Julie and Hib Kinsman, Hib had his rifle leveled at the major's middle, his pale-gray eyes rock hard.

"The lieutenant's key, Major," he said, motioning

with the rifle. "And while you're at it, give me the gold map you have in your pocket."

The Indians reached the bottom of the rise and raced their ponies after the coach, firing rifles and bows as they galloped.

The major's eyes grew penetrating, and there was an odd mockery in them that was matched by a twist to his mouth. "Mister, I don't know how you know I'm carrying it, and not Roark here."

"It's one of those secrets of war that become a headliner. Gold maps always have a way of being as prominent as a new saloon in a church district, no matter what precautions are taken. Your aide's case was much too obvious."

The glint of a rough-and-ready temper showed in the major's quick eyes. "You'll never get it off me. Roark—show him what I mean!"

The trooper flipped back the major's cape that had been kept neatly folded on his lap and brought to view the .44 Starr revolver, over the metal case. His voice was very soft. "It's been pointed at your heart ever since we pulled out of the relay station, mister."

Decklin's body tensed; spread-legged, his arms pinned stiffly behind him, he fought the haze of rage that drifted over him. His voice was level, the words leaping from his lips as he jerked his left shoulder toward the major. "Now's a hell of a time to threaten each other. Turn me loose!"

The coach lurched around a sharp turn, swaying dangerously. Behind it, the Apache guns barked vengefully. The trail lifted around the shoulder of a ragged rise of rocks.

Then all was confusion and shattering chaos. An Apache bullet had taken one of the lead horses in the head. The horse dropped, pulling its teammate down with it.

The other two teams piled into the downed one, kicking and screaming in their tangled harness, fighting to gain their feet. The coach slammed into the twisted mass of horses. It tipped, and then skidded sideways on the narrow trail. A wheel went off the edge, and the coach tilted off the road.

Julie began to scream as the coach pitched forward into nothingness, rolling over three times and pulling the horses off the trail in a screaming tangle, then it came to rest with a thunderous crash against the trunk of an oak.

Screaming, bleeding horses and strewn baggage marked its path from the rim, its yellow wheels spinning crazily in the air. Dust rolled over it in choking clouds as the Apaches swarmed above on the trail, screeching with hate-crazed excitement.

Lieutenant Walker Decklin was conscious, first, of flying wildly into space as his body crashed against the fire-weakened door and he fell free of the tumbling coach. He seemed to be falling forever, sliding down among dirt and rocks. Then he struck something yielding; he twisted his body, groaning with pain from his pinned arms, saw it was the dead horse he had slid into and tried to halt his fall by hooking a leg about its hulk. But he couldn't, and he slid farther down the hill. Branches clawed at his clothing and face, pulled at his arms, which he thought were broken. His head struck something solid and hard.

Blinding pain roared swiftly through him. Glancing above through half-closing eyes, he saw the screeching Apaches holding their mounts on the rim; then he saw the two Confederates on their Appaloosa horses ride up and look down. The men's laughs sounded like something from a bad dream, sinister and frightening.

Decklin tried to turn over on his stomach and slid again down the ravine. Each jolting motion tearing a new agony from his shackled arms.

He was conscious of burning heat, of glittering light and swirling darkness. He glanced up again and saw, rather than heard, the two Confederates urging their horses over the rim, the Apaches on either side of them. He cried out once to warn the others, but his voice was only a whisper in his ears. Then he heard the Confederates' squealing laughs and the Apache screams—heard the thrashing of the downed animals. With an effort, he pulled his face from the ground and watched an Apache slip from his pony and jump on top of the overturned coach.

He watched the Confederates dismounting, saw them pry open the coach door, saw the Indian reach into the coach.

And when the Apache pulled his arm out, the torn fabric of Julie's white lace blouse was clutched in his fist. The Apache yelled a shrill sound, waving the cloth to the rest of the Indians as he dropped his body down into the coach in one bounding swing.

Both Confederates quickly pulled themselves up to the side of the door opening, watching and laughing. Lieutenant Decklin tried to force his body from the ground—what for, he didn't know; he couldn't help. There was nothing Lieutenant Walker Decklin could do. . . . Nothing at all.

So he let his body ease down to the ground; the sharp pains of his hands and arms kept the feeling of being alive stabbing through his body; and now the pain in his head was driving all feeling from him. He began letting himself sink down into the darkness of his dizziness. But then the panic-stricken scream of Julie Booth pierced through that dizziness.

The woman screamed again. He tried working his knees under his body and pushing his body upward by digging into the rocky slope with the point of his shoulder. He pulled his aching body a short three feet up the rise, like a slithering reptile. The scream sounded again, lasting longer than seemed humanly possible; it pushed the light-headedness from his brain. He rose to his feet and let his body sag against the oak.

Great breaths of pain gasped from his lungs.

For a moment he leaned against the tree, tugging on his cuffed wrists behind his back; then he began climbing, scrambling awkwardly among the boulders. The screams of Julie began to come more closely together, till they beat against each other almost continuously, and yet did not diminish in their piercing intensity. He had to hang on to his nerves to keep climbing. He slipped and fell, then began inching himself forward with shoulder tips and knees. Cold perspiration beaded his forehead and ran in rivulets down his face. He looked up and saw that the coach wheels were still spinning.

And he did another foolish thing. He yelled, "Rebel trash!" and saw the Confederates and the Apaches spin at his feeble cry, and did not know whether the Confederate standing on top of the coach or the Indian going through the baggage fired at him, for each instantly slammed a rifle to their shoulder.

He owed Julie this much, to attract attention from her.

The crash of a rifle split the air as he threw himself sideways and slid down among the rocks, the bullet chipping fragments into his blurring eyes. In his clumsy condition, his legs tangled in some gnarled roots and he fell hard; the back of his head hit with violent force against the trunk of the oak. He heard Julie's scream once more, vaguely conscious that the sound had become a hysterical sob; he thought he heard the running thud of footsteps crashing through the brush, coming towards him.

CHAPTER THREE

When Lieutenant Decklin came to, the young night sky was beginning to glow with the jeweled halos of a million saints. The only sound he heard was that of some civic-minded sparrows holding an indignation meeting about the blue jay in a neighboring scrub oak.

He moved and found he was wedged in the crotch of some cedar mesquite. Sharp pains ran up and down his arms. With each slight movement, the pain of his head wound increased.

A gasping groan came from his lips as he worked away from the branches. Not able to use his hands, he slipped to the ground and slid farther down the rocky hillside until he reached bottom. He groaned softly for a few moments, looking up the distance of at least a hundred-odd feet he knew he would have to climb. Pain and exhaustion kept washing through his body.

Gradually he worked himself to his knees, shaking his head like a wounded bear. Listening intently, he heard only the scolding of the blue jay and the chatter of a magpie . . . nothing else.

Pulling his legs under him, he slowly stood.

He looked taller than usual, but the illusion was caused by his thinness. His wool trousers and jacket were torn and his hat lost in the fall. Early moonlight set down on his pathetically awkward scampering as he labored up the slope.

Resting for a moment, he rubbed a bruised chin against his aching left shoulder. Night shadows struck ghostly images about him. He shook his head again, trying to clear the throbbing cobwebs; he should have heard some sound other than his own! But he didn't.

Stumbling, sliding, clawing and pumping with feet and shoulders, he worked up to more level ground.

Stopping, he lay flat against the slope, breath coming in labored gasps. Light sifted through the tree branches, and glancing about, out and across the desert, he could see clearly for fifty miles, and in all that monstrous waste, nothing fluttered or moved.

He arose, his eyes wide, his mouth compressed. One of his cheekbones was skinned; his face was grimy with dirt and cuts.

Moving closer toward the coach, he heard no sound of movement. Strewn baggage had been cut open with knives; apparel of all kinds lay scattered on the ground and ripped into as if somebody had been looking for something particular. No doubt the gold map Mitchel was carrying, Decklin thought, and wondered if the raiders had gotten it. This was no work of Apaches, but a planned raid of the Confederates, using Indians as scapegoats.

He saw the two dead horses, of the six-horse team,

black streaks of dried blood puddled about them.
The four other animals were nowhere in sight. The
driver and guard were lying on their backs; one had
a bullet hole in his neck; the other had died from the
fall.

A stabbing pain pulsed through his chained arms.
"Have to get these cuffs off," he mumbled, stumbling
closer to the overturned coach. ". . . Mitchel . . .
got to get the key . . . He must be inside . . ."

As he peered into the darkened coach, he could
hear breathing and muffled moans. When his eyes
became accustomed to the dark interior, he was able
to make out the crumpled form of Hib. Strange he
should feel a sense of relief that he was alive, when
for the past five years he'd wished him dead, instead
of Susan. A shadow moved at the far end, huddled
against the upside-down door. It was Julie. And the
thought struck him: Since she was still inside the
coach, the odds were that she had only suffered hys-
teria when the Apache had touched her. He glanced
about the shadows. Major Mitchel and Trooper
Roark were not inside.

Knowing he couldn't help Hib or Julie until he
found Mitchel and was freed of his handcuffs, he was
pushing away from the coach when he heard a twig
behind him snap, sounding like a gunshot in the
sickening silence.

Before he could spin around to make a false attempt to defend himself, a voice whispered, "That
. . . you, Lieutenant Decklin?"

The lieutenant flung Major Mitchel a short, bitter

glance as he hauled abruptly around. "Unlock these."

"Your friends in there are all right," mumbled the major, stepping forward and working a key into the cuffs' lock. "Thought it best to leave them there for the time being, until I saw if the Indians had left."

Rubbing circulation into his raw wrists and painfully flexing his arms, Walker Decklin turned to face the major. "See the Confederates?"

"No—oo." Drawled surprised was in Mitchel's voice. "You continue to insist this was the work of Confederates?"

"I do. I saw them," Decklin said softly. "It's my guess that's the only reason we're standing here. They must have convinced the Apaches our scalps weren't worth the trouble."

"If what you say is true, they must have had a good persuasive."

"Guns, no doubt. Where's Roark?"

The major evaded the question. "I looked for you . . . but as you can see, it's obvious I didn't find you."

Walker Decklin turned and looked at the major with watchful steadiness. "Roark's dead," he said indignantly.

Mitchel's head was as still as a stone-head on a column, fixed to look one way. "I gave Trooper Roark one of the two best horses. . . . I hid the others down below. He should reach Colonel Moore's headquarters, outside Stillwater, within three days."

"You did *what?* Fort Ward's two hundred and fifty miles closer!" Decklin turned a little pale with the fury bottled up in him. "Why? You lost your marbles, sir? If those Apaches decide to come back . . ."

"Lieutenant," Mitchel said stiffly, "I don't have to answer to you. The winning of this war is what counts! Not just a few lives."

Walker Decklin took a deep breath. "Meaning, Roark has that gold map?"

Major Mitchel lowered his head; his hands went to his left thigh, and he said in a weak, low voice, "Lord, that hurts."

Decklin saw a deep crimson stain spreading across the major's leg, the blood slowly trickling through his fingers. "Shot?"

Mitchel took a deep breath and peered up at him. "A piece of metal from the coach ran through me when we went over, but I'll not be asking any favors from the likes of you."

Decklin grinned to himself, and took a step forward. "Let me see how bad it is."

But before he could examine the major, shuffling noise at the coach's broken door turned his head. He saw Hib Kinsman's face level with his, a ragged gash on his temple. Then Hib was pushing the whimpering and limp Julie out of the opening.

"Take her," he said to Decklin. But the lieutenant found his cramped arms couldn't hold her weight. Major Mitchel limped over and helped the woman to the ground.

Decklin said, "She's all right, Hib?"

"Shook up and scared . . . that's all."

Bending over Julie, Decklin called up to Hib: "See if you can find my satchel inside."

Mitchel grumbled, "Horse medicine for humans?"

Decklin said mildly, "Why not? Horses, hounds, or humans—they amout to the same." He took his veterinary case from Hib Kinsman as the man jumped down from the coach. Then, muttering to himself, he calmly stated, "I don't know how we'll do it . . . but we can try and patch up the horses to see us to Fort Ward." He winced at the agony of his strained arms when he tried to move Julie.

"Don't count on that," said Hib Kinsman, taking a deep breath and planting his feet firmly before Decklin.

Lieutenant Decklin looked up, surprise on his face.

The two men stared at each other, and Decklin knew the thing tormenting the big man: the gold map.

"Don't be crazy, Hib. Roark's got a head start."

Hib Kinsman's voice was a thin, shallow sound striking out at him. "My obligation to you is over, Walk," he said. "You can trot away from here a free man. If *anything,* you owe me something. Which way did Roark go?"

"You'll never get away with it," warned Mitchel, slipping to the ground, clutching his thigh and cursing it. "A civilian stealing from the Union can be a serious offense."

"No more so than a lieutenant's." Hib Kinsman

grinned down at Decklin. "Ah, come with me, Walk. We can both make it double on the sound horse. Nothing has come between us."

Decklin slowly rose. "What I did is nothing compared to what you're going to do."

Hib said shortly, "You stole three thousand dollars from the Union . . ."

"Borrowed," interrupted Lieutenant Decklin. "I intend to pay it back."

Hib laughed. "It amounts to the same thing."

Decklin shook his head. "Not in my book. That money was for a kid's operation—something we were both responsible for."

"It was an accident," said Hib in a cold, flat voice. "Joel walked into our line of fire . . ."

Decklin's gaze ran right into Hib Kinsman's stare. "We were told to quit rifle practice . . . but no, we had to sneak the rifles out behind the barn . . ." Decklin paused, watching the steely coldness of the man's eyes that seemed to transfix him. "Oh—what's the use?"

Hib Kinsman flushed; his fingers came in contact with the gun at his side. Then all sense of shame was gone and he flashed the gun from its holster.

"I didn't want it this way," Hib said, leveling the weapon at Decklin.

"What about Julie? You leaving her?"

"She'll understand."

"She might, but I won't." Decklin let a short space of silence break into his words, then continued. ". . . or maybe I will." There was a touch of challenge in his steady eyes, the immobile thin mouth. "I might want to stop you," Decklin softly said. "There's only one sound horse left from the teams . . . and that horse is *my* only way of getting to Fort Ward."

Hib grinned, "You sure want to get there bad enough." He took another backward step, as the lieutenant took a step forward, and raised the revolver until its bore was in line with the tip of Walker Decklin's left shoulder. "Why?"

"I don't think you'd understand. Or would you? Joel's there . . . I'm to meet him."

"Oh, I get it. Still your brother's keeper." Hib cocked his head to the side and laughed. "So—oo, you still have conscience trouble."

"Yes . . . there is such a thing, and I happen to have it," Decklin replied, taking another step closer to the man, fury making his voice thick. "But I know *you* don't."

"Keep back, Walk," warned Hib. "I don't want to, but I'll wing you if I have to."

Mitchel made a clumsy attempt to unholster his gun, only to have Hib Kinsman step over and toe it from him, pick it up, and jam it into his belt.

Mitchel's gaze moved from the lieutenant to the civilian. He looked now at the lieutenant and said, "Stop him."

"What'll I do? Spit bullets at him?"

Major Mitchel maintained his composure admirably. "If you don't try, Lieutenant, you'll be an accessory to what he plans. You've fought for the Union

. . . know the meaning of what we're fighting for. This man is after the gold map for *himself*. He has no cause other than his own greed."

Decklin rubbed the palm of his hand against his right thigh, missing the gun that usually hung there. He shook his head. "I'm not that crazy, sir. Anyway, *sir*, I don't owe you a thing." He held out his hands so the major could see the crimson, raw cuts from the handcuffs on his wrists. "Make those marks and their pain disappear, Major Mitchel, and we might be in business."

The major's voice was grim. "Remember, Lieutenant Decklin, a man's conscience is his fort, and he alone can make a Hell out of it. If you don't want to listen to me, listen to your conscience. Hell is over-populated by men who never took the time to lend an ear to their conscience."

Hib grunted, "You sound like you've been there, Major Mitchel."

"What do you think it takes to make a major? "Well, Lieutenant . . . I know you have a conscience. What are you going to do about this man?"

Turning, Walker Decklin spoke with a slow and easy tone. "Don't talk to me about a man's conscience, sir. I know a lot about it—maybe too much, if that's possible."

Hib Kinsman's sarcastic laughter came like the crackling sound of pine cones in a fire. "Maybe the lieutenant is finding out that a man's conscience can be useful as a dead horse." He laughed again, the noise of it sounding like fingernails rubbed over rough sandpaper.

"You won't catch up with Trooper Roark," said Mitchel, brushing a hand across his eyes. "He's been gone for over three hours."

"Men leave trails," replied Hib, backing over to the half-skittish bay gelding hidden in the brush. He began fumbling with the harness with one hand, all the while keeping his gun leveled at them with his right hand.

Decklin gritted his teeth. He hated asking it, yet he did. "If something goes wrong with Joel at Fort Ward, see that the kid gets another try—another doctor . . ."

"You sound like I'm leaving you to the Apaches," Hib muttered. "They won't be back. And you can shank-mare it into Fort Ward if you can't patch up the other horses."

"You're pretty sure about those Apaches, aren't you?"

Hib nodded. "Pretty sure—but not positive." Then his jaws clenched and he asked again, "Won't you come with me, Walk? Don't be a fool and stay." He watched Walker Decklin shake his head. "Someday you'll forget about Joel and your conscience. *Gold,* Walk—*gold* is what counts!"

"Lieutenant Decklin," came Major Mitchel's demanding voice, "stop that man!"

But Lieutenant Walker Decklin stood quiet and watched Hib Kinsman vault on the bay's bare back and lope off, plowing his path through the grass. There was a strange hurt in his face as he said, "If I tried to stop him," his voice hardly above a whisper, "how do you think you and the girl would have gotten out of here?"

"You *could* have tried," said Major Mitchel.

"I *could* be dead."

CHAPTER FOUR

Morning came without preamble, leaping over the horizon and destroying the darkness with dazzling suddenness. The cantaloupe-colored flame of the sun splashed across the ravine-cut country, chasing shadows down before it.

Walker Decklin, clutching the stage guard's rifle and leading the limping chestnut that Major Mitchel and Julie rode, pulled on the reins. Harness leather creaked against the strain as he surveyed the expanse across which they had traveled all night.

Off in the distance the shape of a town took on form, hanging like a great wooden jewel, not sparkling but palpitating in the early heat haze.

Satisfied that there was no one in sight, Decklin motioned for them to dismount.

The chestnut stood with wobbly legs spread wide, head low. The scarlet gash on his near fore shoulder cut down across his chest. A quick stitching of the wound and spread of ointment had made the animal vaguely suitable for travel. The others had to be put out of their misery.

When Mitchel continued to stay mounted, in the rigid form of an indignant general, Decklin said,

49

"Climb down." It was an order, not an invitation. "No sense in killing this poor animal. And for sure, all of us can't ride into Fort Ward on him."

"Meaning you are?" Mitchel's face paled more from rising anger than from loss of blood.

Decklin nodded. "This close, I'd be a fool not to. You can't stop me and you can't stop me from riding out of there." He patted the rifle stock confidently.

"You want me to believe *you* aren't interested in locating Roark and that gold map?" Major Mitchel's voice was something Decklin could not remember: harsh, low, and trembling with repressed rage. "And I guess you think I ought to thank you for patching me up . . . getting this animal on its feet . . . getting us this far . . ."

"Nope," Decklin interrupted, the muscles of his face clenching. "I only want to get to Doc Gordon's office, find out about my brother, then leave. Nothing else. Believe me or don't. Now get down."

"Can't I come with you?" asked Julie.

Suddenly and abruptly came the faint brassy blast of a bugle blaring across the prairie, its sound coming from outside the town of Fort Ward.

Decklin spun around. The dry wind of Oklahoma swept tiny dust devils about his boots. He could detect pinpoints of movement and horses the size of prairie dogs. His eyes narrowed. It was a regiment.

Mitchel put a hand to his eyes, shielding them from the sun. "See there," he hastily said, pointing with a hand, "over to the left. The flag! It's *Confederate!*"

Decklin whistled like a butcher-bird, without melody. "The Rebs have taken over Fort Ward."

Major Mitchel's laugh was like the roar of a cornered lion. He looked down at the lieutenant. "Still going in?"

"I am."

"Your conscience must really bother you."

"You tagged it right when you called it *Fort Hell*."

"You're a fool."

"I am. One who has made Fort Hell his home," Decklin agreed sarcastically. "Now let's move out of sight." He led the chestnut closer to some sagebrush that had piled up against the shallow ravine.

"Please, Walk," Julie said again, "take me with you." Bright sunlight played tricky shadows on her soiled face. "Please."

Decklin looked up at her and shrugged. "I'm sure Hib will find a way to send for you."

"He had no right to leave me back there!"

"You afraid he'll get the gold map and really *forget* you?"

"He wouldn't dare!"

"I thought you and Hib were going to be married."

"I just said that," she replied casually. A smile struck upon her face, a smile as glitteringly chilled as a gleam of light on the edge of a sword. She said, "Walk, I thought you didn't care."

"I don't."

He watched her slide off the chestnut's bare back. Without bothering to help, he watched her flex her legs like a ballerina. Anger was growing again in him, knowing now why she and Hib were on the stage. He looked at her, slightly shaking his head. In the cool glare of dawn, the pale skin of her face looked dry and drawn. Her lips were a thin, brittle line and her eyes kept staring at him. She moved closer.

"Don't let me stay here, Walk," she said softly, tipping back her head. The brilliant sun struck full on her features. She fluttered her lashes as she looked up at him and came closer.

"The sun is in my eyes," she cooed.

"Well?"

"Make a shadow."

The controlled patience in him was a thin veneer. Abruptly, it cracked wide open. He reached out and caught her arms and brought her to him.

Her eyes half closed. He made a sound deep in his throat and drew her tight against him. She met his lips fully.

Sharply he released her. Stepping back, he snapped a glance at the major seated on the chestnut and said curtly to the woman, "It's no use, Julie . . . it'll never work. We nearly tried it before." He was staring down at her with a strange expression on his face. "That would have been nice, though," he said almost angrily, "if you hadn't done it for your own purpose!"

"It's still a MacKay, isn't it? If you couldn't have Susan, her sister Aldis will do. That stupid, back-hills Aldis MacKay!"

"I never knew a MacKay to be a conniver."

Without warning, she had her arms about his neck, forcing her lips against his. And he heard her saying, "Walk, you'll have to ride a long trail to find a woman who can kiss you like that. Even a MacKay."

He took her arms from around his neck. "I'm not taking you with me."

"You owe me something, Walk," she said.

"Now's not the time to collect."

He turned his back to her and motioned with his rifle for the major to dismount. Keeping a tight hold on the chestnut and rifle, he used his left hand to help the man down. Once on the ground he adjusted the major's makeshift bandage, took out a few tools from his veterinary case he had tied to the harness and lashed them together and pushed them into his pocket. During this time, Major Mitchel did not utter one word.

"You'll be safe here, until night," Decklin told him.

The major found his voice. "Without a horse?"

Decklin ignored him. "You might find use for some of the medicine in there," he said, tossing his case down beside the major.

"Don't overdo your kindness," snapped Mitchel, letting out a breath that fluttered his nostrils. "I hope the Confederates get you."

Decklin shrugged. "I don't," he muttered, and turned to examine the gelding's chest. Seeing he could do nothing further for the animal, he vaulted on the horse's back. It was an awkward mount, for his arms still give him trouble. He pulled the chestnut off to the side, and waited until the animal got its balance.

Cradling the rifle across his lap, he gave Julie a look that offered pity, but no regrets. "Maybe it won't be too long before I can repay you for what you tried," he told her. Then, looking at the major, the softness left his voice: "Those Confederates are *your* handcuffs now, Major. You see how it feels to be bogged down in chains."

Lightly he touched heels to the gelding and moved out toward a rise of clumped rocks.

After turning the chestnut loose at the bottom of a grass-filled ravine, Decklin worked his way into town on foot.

The air was becoming warmer, and the cotton-woods, a block over on the residential street, rustled in the breeze. Decklin edged tighter to the trees, seeing four Confederates bulge onto the street, whipping up their horses to a fast run. Their rebel yells and gunshots sent what few townfolk braved the main street of Fort Ward scampering for cover.

Against the eastern sky, Decklin saw the spire of a church, topped with a small white cross. He straightened his thin body and looked much older than he really was. Big in shoulders and chest, with lean saddle legs, the touch of frost at the temples would have given his sun-tanned complexion a dignified look if his face were not set so grim.

Only once before had he been in Fort Ward. That was when he made arrangements with Doc Gordon, two months ago.

He moved slowly from the cottonwood shadows, making sure no Confederates huddled about. They all seemed to have assembled at the western end of town: a body of more than 150 men.

Lieutenant Walker Decklin came to the first establishment, now vacant of sound.

Cautiously he worked toward the rear of the buildings. Here was a narrow alley, cluttered with boxes, barrels, and hay bales. There was a mingled smell of cedarwood smoke and frying meat in the air about the café, sharpening his senses to such a degree that warm water found its way into his mouth. He didn't know when he last had eaten, and he had to brush the back of his hand across his lips to keep the trickle of water confined to his mouth.

Gripping the stock of the rifle, he went on. If recollection served correct, first would be the barbershop . . . the bakery . . . Millie's Millinery . . . the cafe . . . the general store. Doc Gordon's would be the small office beside the store, partly hidden from view around the corner.

The pound of hoofbeats racing down the alley spun him around. Then came the yells of those four Confederates.

In his haste not to be discovered, he twisted around too quickly and slammed into a tin garbage can outside the back door of the general store.

Somewhere farther down the alley a dog barked and ran in search of the clattering racket.

"See who's down there," Decklin heard a Confederate call out. "Maybe it's another Blue Belly! If it is, shoot him!"

Lieutenant Decklin burst into a full run for Doc Gordon's. He dashed around the corner—and stopped as if he had slammed into a brick wall. A swift blaze of fury raced through him at seeing the two familiar Appaloosas . . . the same two dappled blue roans, with a creamy blanket of lighter spots over their rumps, that were back at the Apache raid when the stagecoach turned over. Burned into the leather skirts of the saddles were the initials: C. S. A. Confederate States of America.

Gritting his teeth, he pulled himself up against the wall and flattened there among the boxes and barrels piled at least eight feet high.

The riders were passing the bakery. He heard one laugh. "Colonel Viking sure don't want prisoners taken . . . takes too much to feed 'em."

Decklin knew he had to make his move, and make it fast.

He had just decided to take his chances hiding behind the cluttered boxes, when he heard the squeaky hinge of Doc Gordon's screen door push open.

He craned his neck around the edge of the boxes, and saw, framed in the doorway, a gray-coated Confederate—a sandy, heavy-pore-faced man that took up all the space in the archway with his two hundred forty pounds of pure muscle. The man stretched his arms and let an enormous yawn cut his face. With long strides, he walked to the Appaloosa.

A radiance of anger ran over Decklin like summer lightning as he remembered what this man had done. Steadily the hoofbeats poured closer to the doctor's office, their sound echoing shrilly down the alley.

Giving it no further thought, Decklin leaped through the gap in the piled boxes and barrels, raising his rifle stock. The Confederate whirled at his noise. In the man's surprise, his mouth kept flapping open and shut like a fish out of water, with no sound escaping.

Decklin brought the rifle down with a healthy swipe on the man's neck. There was a dull *snick* and the man in gray went limp. Quickly Decklin grabbed him by the arms before he fell, and pulled him behind the boxes. He wanted to get the man's hand gun, but time was extremely limited; he didn't try for it.

With a leap, Decklin kicked open the doctor's door and pushed it shut with his sagging body, just as the four whooping Confederates came abreast of the building and slammed into the main street again.

The tinkling of a glass phial crashing to the wooden floor brought Decklin's body from the door; His rifle came up in a rapid movement of both his arms. He took the room in with a sweeping glance.

Drawing a deep sigh, he lowered the rifle and pushed an arm across his sweat-beaded forehead.

"Hi, Doc," he mumbled, looking at the little man in a tan knee-length smock. Then the lieutenant was attracted to the patient on the couch. The man lying there was a replica of the Confederate he had just clobbered. A scarlet-blotched rag was bound about his head, his eyes closed.

The doctor's face was all smiles as he moved from his patient and extended his hand. "You startled me, Lieutenant Decklin."

As Decklin shook the offered hand, he could feel the strength of the man, no matter how small he was, pour through those fingers. The sweetish smell of chloroform from the broken phial began filling the room. Decklin coughed.

The doctor went to the window. "Here, I'll let some fresh air in."

". . . don't . . ." coughed Decklin.

The old man saw the tension lines on Decklin's face, and the smile on his face sobered. "They after you?"

"I wear a blue uniform."

"What did you do with Given Holly?"

"If you mean the fellow that just left here . . . he'll be out for a while." Decklin moved across the room, past the lone table in the middle of the floor, headed for the closet at the far side of the room, big enough to hide a man. With a sudden jerk, he pulled open the door. Satisfied that nobody else was in the single room, he went back to the man on the couch. Inspecting the man with amazed eyes, he said, "He looks just like the man I clipped."

"This one is Gills Holly—one of the Holly twins. You just tangled with his brother. They're mean

ones . . . part of that Colonel Viking's bunch. Rode
in here before dawn, took the town by surprise and
left me this—" He pointed a finger at the couch.
"Gills's head must be made of stone. An ordinary
man should be dead."

Uninterested, Decklin drawled, "Where's Joel?"

"Your brother didn't come."

"Why? I gave him the three thousand dollars for
the operation. What happened?" Decklin's eyes slitted. "Did you *up* your price again?"

A huff of anger came to the doctor's voice. "No, I
did not. But it seems your brother don't mind his
limping, when he can pick up two thousand head of
Texas longhorns for three thousand . . ."

"What are you talking about," interrupted Decklin.

"Here," said the doctor, going to the table and
pulling open a small drawer. He reached back in the
drawer and rummaged among some articles. Then he
handed Decklin a small crumpled piece of paper.
"Sorry I opened it," he said, "but the letter was ad-
dressed to me."

Walker Decklin snatched it from him, reading it
half aloud.

"Walk, I got a great chance to start the cattle
ranch we've dreamed about. I'm using the $3,-
000 to buy out old man Hertzler's cows. It might
sound crazy to you, a cripple doing this, and
longhorns plentiful as fleas on a hound. But
Walk, on a horse I don't even know I'm a

cripple, and this is my chance to make something of myself. I'll wait the herd here in Texas for you . . . for three weeks. Then I'm hirin' me a bunch of riders and we're trailin' the herd to Kansas City. Still sound crazy? Not to me, because I can get us $40 a head for every longhorn delivered there. I know you've saved all your money to get my operation. It's stupid to say thanks, so I won't. I can say it better by getting us started in the cattle business. I'll see you the second week of April."

Your brother Joel

For a long silent moment, Decklin stared at the scribbling. Then he grinned with regret. Joel had really believed him when he told the kid he had been discharged. He grunted under his breath, "Three weeks can be a long time, Joel." And then his mind was carried away with memories. Ever since he could remember, Joel had wanted a cattle ranch. Decklin shook his head. The thought of Joel using the money for cattle didn't set right with Walker Decklin's conscience; but if Joel had used the money for his operation, that was a horse of a different color. Crumpling the letter into a ball, he threw it to the floor.

"That kid is crazy! There's no cattle trails going north! Even so . . . the Confederates won't let him outa Texas!"

"It must run in the family," said the doctor.

Decklin flashed up his eyes. "Meanin' what?"

"You've let your brother believe you have been

discharged . . . let him believe that money was
yours. . . ."

"What makes you think differently?"

"It's obvious as a ruptured appendix."

Decklin lowered his eyes and slumped into the
chair beside the table. "You're a foxy one." He put
his free hand across his eyes, muttering, "What do
you do with a kid like that?" and unknowingly let his
rifle sink to the floor.

Just then the screen door squeaked and the
paneled door leading into the room banged open.

Walker Decklin was on his feet in an instant.

Framed in the doorway was the Confederate Decklin had just knocked out, blood streaming down his
jaw and neck. He stood there, dazed and swaying on
his feet, the gun still in his holster.

The doctor took a deep breath and said, "Told you
those Holly twins got thick skulls."

Not giving the Confederate a chance to gather his
senses, Decklin threw himself bodily at the man's
knees. He felt his body jackknife about the Confederate's legs. They went down in a tumble of arms and
legs, both going for the hand-gun at the Confederate's side. The man tried to grapple him and Decklin
freed the gun and hit him in the face with it, only to
lose it in the shuffle.

Free to rise, he was not yet off his knees when he
looked toward the door and saw those four searching
Confederates coming into the room.

Desperately Decklin made a grab for his rifle, only
to have it kicked from his hands.

Frustration, humiliation, anger—all the pent-up emotions within Walker Decklin—rose to the surface.

A big Confederate snorted contemptuously, "Now we got you, Yankee," and charged forward.

An awesome sense of utter helplessness robbed Decklin of stamina. Yet he found the strength to rise to his feet, diving for the man's middle. Decklin heard the Confederate's breath leave him with the sudden jolt. Dazed himself from hitting so heavily, Decklin pawed for the man's gun. He didn't make it; the three others were pushing his face into the plank floor and using their boots on him. Blackness began to kill the sunlight . . . the room spun in crazy circles.

"That's enough," said a soft, drawling voice somewhere near the door. "Let him get to his feet. Back off!"

The broken glass of the chloroform phial made a gritty crunch beneath Walker Decklin's boots as he pulled himself to his feet. He lifted himself to a standing position, hands on the table top and halfway folded over it. Raising his head, he could see now what had quieted down the killing rage in the Confederates. Hib Kinsman stood just inside the front door, and the .44 in his hand looked like a cannon, his cream-colored suit dirtier and more torn than when he had last seen him.

Hib grinned. "I see you can still use my help."

CHAPTER FIVE

"Okay, Walk," drawled Hib, "can you make it?"

Decklin nodded. "I think so," he replied, straightening.

"Let's go, then!" snapped Hib, the commanding tone in his voice, as well as the .44, keeping the Confederates under control.

Walker Decklin stooped, picked up his rifle and the fallen hand gun. He was in the act of disarming the Confederates, when Hib Kinsman said, "Don't bother. Let's move out," and jerked his head to the door.

There was no sign of uneasiness about Hib Kinsman, or about the manner in which he kept his .44 leveled at the Confederates. With a gun in his hand, Hib Kinsman was ten feet tall, and if he wanted to, he would defy a regiment if the need arose.

Hib took a backward step, keeping the Confederates covered with his gun, and his boot crunched on a ball of crumpled paper. He glanced down; curiosity made him pick it up. It was Joel's letter. He gave it a swift reading and followed Decklin from the room; but not before he faced the Confederates and spoke to them in a gentle tone that was quiet, steady, inflexible.

"I'm riding out of here . . . and there's not a one of you that will follow. Understand?"

Farther down the alley, he saw Decklin already mounted on one of the Confederate's bay horses, and holding a skittish sorrel.

Hib walked over to him, holding up the crumpled letter. A half-smile hovered around his lips as he said, "I see the kid hasn't eased your conscience." He laughed lightly, holstering his gun, and dropped the letter to the dirt.

"Why'd you come here?" Decklin asked, watching Hib swing into the saddle. "You still want me to believe you haven't got a conscience about Joel? That's why you're here. You wanted to make sure the kid was all right."

"Wrong," Hib replied, "I came back for the gold man. I knew you'd be here and tell me what happened to Mitchel." He smiled now. "You see . . . my conscience never bothers me. I have none. Satisfied?"

Decklin's face darkened. "I was a fool," he said, "to have thought you'd think of anybody other than yourself. I doubt if I'll ever really know you."

"I doubt it, too," Hib said with a smile.

"What happened to Roark?" asked Decklin. "He was supposed to be carryin' . . ."

"Your Major Mitchel is a wise old coot. He tied a dead Roark on a horse, with a cactus barb stuck under the saddle. Had a heck of a time catchin' him!"

He hipped around on the sorrel, glancing swiftly about.

"The Confederates are at the other end of town," said Walker Decklin, backing the bay from the hitch-rack.

"Well, then, let's show this place our dust."

They put their horses at a fast gallop and rode out of Fort Ward.

The dislikes Decklin had nurtured toward Hib these past five years, about Susan, were speedily entering banishment. But there would always be that discord between them about Joel's accident.

Without realizing it, Decklin had pointed his bay into the rough-cut ravines where he'd left Major Mitchel and Julie.

Once there among the boulders, they read signs of chipped rocks and the droppings of many horses. Decklin dismounted, hunkered down to finger the bloody rag that had been Mitchel's bandage.

Hib tossed his right leg over the saddle and came down flat-footed on the ground, both feet striking at the same time. He walked over to stand above Decklin.

"Captured," mumbled Decklin coldly, and he began feeling a sense of regret.

"Not likely," said Hib, reaching down and picking up a Union-issued saddle blanket. Dropping it with a disgusted grunt, he added, "I'd say they were picked up by some Unionists. Those devils are hidden 'round these plains like lice."

"You know a lot about their movements."

Hib Kinsman went to his sorrel and fumbled with the canteen slung on the saddle. Unscrewing the cap, he drank thirstily. When he lowered the canteen and wiped his mouth with the dusty back of his hand, he saw Decklin studying him.

"How else do you think I was able to save your neck?"

"A lot you care about my neck!" gritted Decklin.

"You could say that. And again you couldn't." Hib grinned. "You just gotta get me in the right mood." His grin leaped into loud laughter as he tossed the canteen to Decklin. "Have a drink," he said. "It'll make you feel better."

Decklin caught it and threw it to the ground. "You've lost your hand-hold on that map now. And I'm glad!"

"Ah," said Hib in cooing mockness, "don't say things you don't mean, Walk my boy. You should know me a little by now. If my recollections serve right, Mitchel and his Union boys will head for Colonel Moore's headquarters at Stillwater."

"Meanin'?"

"Obvious. I got to get there!"

"Haven't you forgot something?"

"What?"

"Julie."

Hib laughed. "She'll be where that map is, or I don't know good ole Julie."

Decklin turned his back and walked away; coming to a boulder, he rested against it for a second, then slid his body to the ground, his back resting along the rock. Hib started toward him. Decklin took the handgun from his belt—the one he had picked up from the Confederates at Fort Ward—and aimed it at Hib Kinsman's left knee. A strange deliberateness tightened his features.

"Stay there, Hib," he said.

Hib stopped, but kept grinning down at him. "Scared of me, Walk? What for? Still nursing a grudge about what happened to Susan?"

"She was dead wrong to try and change your kind of livin'."

"She thought I needed her more'n you."

"And you didn't?"

"Not the way you mean."

"You rotten . . ." Decklin's hand tightened on the gun and Hib Kinsman could see anger slam into his face.

"Ah come on, Walk, listen to me. Put the gun down. You look foolish aiming it at me. We both know you haven't got it in you to pull the trigger . . ."

"You're tryin' hard to find out."

Hib Kinsman suddenly dropped his arms. "You've never gave me a chance to explain how things with Susan really were . . ."

"Don't try. It'd only be a lie to suit yourself."

"Take it for what it is. Susan and I was happy . . . far as that goes. She had just told me we were going to have a baby . . ."

Walker Decklin's body stiffened, then he drew up

his legs until his knees were level with his chest. It was there, on those knobby knees, that he rested the barrel of his gun, still keeping it pointed at Hib.

"You didn't know that, I see," said Hib. "Well, now you do." He continued: "Then came that gun-happy, rep-huntin' kid who pulled his pistol on me . . . he was drunk . . . I was unarmed. Susan knew I wasn't carryin' a gun . . . thinking to stop the kid, she jumped between us." Hib Kinsman lowered his eyelids. "She died in my arms . . ."

Decklin said softly, "You expect me to buy that?"

Hib looked up, eyes slitted. "It's off my chest. I don't care if you do, or don't. The main thing now is that map. Susan's dead. Let the dead stay buried."

"Just what's so important about that map?"

"Interested in it now?"

Decklin rubbed his left hand along the cold barrel of his gun, but did not take it off Hib Kinsman. "I don't know," he muttered. "I just don't know."

Hib's conniving was sharpened. "Listen, Walk . . . that map tells what route a Union wagon train is takin', coming from the gold fields of Nevada. They're carrying over a million dollars in gold bars . . ."

"Whew . . ."

"Buy a lot of cattle for Joel's ranch. . . . Half of it's yours . . . you can buy a mighty good-sized piece of real estate. How about it? Let's ride into Stillwater."

Walker Decklin was staring down at his boots. Then he stretched out his legs until they were flat against the ground. The hand with the gun in it went there, too. "I just don't know," he mumbled. "I just don't know," he said again, and looked over at the canteen he had thrown to the dirt. "I'll take that drink now."

Hib Kinsman went over to it, picked it up and brought the container over to Decklin. "I knew, if I waited long enough, you'd come over to my way of thinkin'."

Wiping his mouth with the back of his bruised hand, Walker Decklin pulled himself to his feet and housed his gun in his belt. He stood and looked back toward Fort Ward. "Why aren't you worried about them comin' after us?"

"Nothing to worry about."

"Sure?"

"Sure. What would those gray cruds want with us?"

Decklin turned to face him. "What did you call them?"

"Cruds. Means a bunch of nothing. Now how about it, Walk? I don't want to wait around all day . . . I want to get long gone for Stillwater. Let's move out."

Decklin's empty stomach ground in on his backbone. His bones, bruised by the wreck, and the fight, felt as if they were pulling loose from their anchoring muscles. His head began swimming from lack of sleep.

Hib Kinsman, more than nine years his senior, looked none the worse for wear. Walker Decklin ex-

perienced a twinge of jealousy. Was his own tiredness
caused by the fact that there was nothing to forge him
on, as Hib's greed was sustaining him?

Then the thought struck him. Hib had gotten him
out of a couple of tough scrapes within the past
twenty-four hours . . . he hated to be obligated to
the man. If he could make it to Stillwater before
Hib, warn Colonel Moore, it might just stop Hib
from doing something he'd be sorry for
later . . . and in the same instant, it could help
things go easy at his own court-martial.

He put a hand to his eyes, and the thoughts within
his brain made him dizzy until he swayed on his feet.

Hib put a hand out to him. "You better sit down
again," and helped ease him to the ground. "What's
the matter? Are you sick? Can I get you something?"

"Yes, you can—a new conscience."

Hib Kinsman tensed as if Decklin had slapped his
face. Then he stood and said, "Now you listen to me,
Walk. I'll give you one minute either to buck loose
of your conscience, or you can stay here and rot with
it in your lap!"

Without raising his head, Walker Decklin said,
gently, "Go on . . . I'll catch up."

"Sure you want it that way?"

Decklin gave a small nod. He had to have a few
moments by himself to think it out.

Walker Decklin sat watching a man who admitted
he had *no* conscience ride off full of assurance he already had a million dollars. And here he sat, a man
whose conscience was tender as a baby's fingertips,

and working to make a dollar was like trying to scratch his ear with his elbow. . . . A great loneliness overwhelmed him, and Decklin's confused state of mind became suddenly clear.

He jumped to his feet, ran to his horse, jerked at the cinch, and, without using the stirrups, vaulted into the saddle.

He half-said to himself, "Right or wrong . . . I'll do it."

CHAPTER SIX

For two days, Decklin continued to ride east toward Camp Stillwater. He had made his choice and promised himself to keep it. The Oklahoma plains furnished him his only food within four days. A meat-scarce jackrabbit, tough as a boot sole.

Topping the shallow crown of a hill, he rested his horse on the brim and looked down at a ribbon-winding stream. The hill sloped off to the north, belly-deep with late March grass. He kneed the bay to the water and refreshed himself, refilled his canteen, drank his supper and let the horse graze for half an hour.

The early evening sky was crystal clear. The air touched his face like a mental tonic. He looked to the hills humping the eastern horizon. If he kept to the high country and took the short cut to Stillwater, he just might make it there before Hib.

He mounted, neck-reining into the hills.

Night found a few wispy black clouds forming a frown across the face of the coltish moon; dawn foaled over the plains like a weak-kneed filly, getting up for the first time. The pale light found him still in the saddle and a fragile rain had come and gone, leaving clusters of diamond drops sparkling on the grass.

Giving the bay its head to climb the next rise, he gazed down on the flat-bowled valley and strung-out, mushroomed camp of Stillwater. Pup tents lined up like cultivated pumpkins. The camel-backed, tree-fuzzed rises to the East made a perfect screen for any enemy.

Miserably raking fingers through his damp hair, he started to lope down the ridge. Suddenly movement among the trees at the far side of the camp caught his attention. He sat back in the saddle, pulling on the reins.

Narrowing his eyes, he caught the shine of metal trappings—the forms of riders lining up, stirrup to stirrup, hidden from the view of Camp Stillwater. Even in the false light, he knew he was witnessing the assembly of a large body of Confederates.

Knowing he had the advantage to warn the Unionists, without a further thought to his own safety, he slammed home his heels. The head-hanging bay leaped forward as if shot.

Galloping straight for the lone sentry leaning against a cannon-smashed cottonwood, chin resting on his chest, dozing, Decklin yelled, "Make ready for attack . . ." Decklin kept waving his hand and calling: "Confederates coming! Attack! *Attack!*"

The sleepy-eyed sentry snapped to attention, rifle jerking up. "Who . . . who goes there?" the man mumbled in a sleep-thick voice.

"Sound assembly . . . Confederates are over

there!" Decklin flung his hand toward the trees and hauled back on the reins. Urgency was in his voice. "Is Major Mitchel here?"

"Rode in yesterday . . . but . . . but . . ." The man couldn't focus his foggy brain.

"Point out Colonel Moore's tent."

The sentry was pulling a hand slowly across his eyes, a wide yawn cutting across his face. Decklin reached down and grabbed a handful of the man's jacket front; his anger grew loud. "Man, hurry it up. Take much longer and you're headed for a mighty long sleep!"

"There . . . over there," mumbled the sentry, leveling a finger at the largest canvas tent in the center of the smaller ones, lamp glow shining a feeble orange color from its interior. "But . . . but who are you . . . I can't let you pass . . ."

Decklin twisted the man's jacket in his fist and gave it a vicious shake. "You fool!" he growled. "Don't you understand? Get your bugler to sound *attack!*" He gave the sentry a push and spun the bay on a dime, racing for Colonel Moore's tent. If the sentry wouldn't listen to reason, the colonel would have to. He jumped his tired horse over camp clutter, the bay's hoofs barely missing sleep-wobbly Unionists tumbling from bedrolls, cursing the racket he was making.

His horse was still hock-sliding to a stop when his boots struck dirt. He jerked Colonel Moore's tent flap aside without bothering to announce himself.

Immediately someone extinguished the lamp, and he stumbled inside.

"Colonel Moore, is that you?" Decklin anxiously asked, falling against a small wood table that was already overturned. "I know someone's in here . . . who is it?" He heard the canvas rip at the far end of the darkened tent; vaguely he caught the form of a man jumping through the cut opening and felt the swish of a knife slinging past his right ear.

Instinctively, he ducked and fell to all fours, hand reaching for his gun. Abruptly the brassy blare of a bugle sounding its duty call pierced the air, with the rallying call of: *"Attack!"* At once the camp was a wild confusion of men, horses, and gunfire.

The knife-thrower had vanished before Decklin had time to send a shot after him. Getting to his feet, he stumbled against something soft. Reaching down, his searching hands felt it was a body. His fingers came away sticky and warm; the man had been stabbed in the back.

Eyes becoming accustomed to the half-darkness, he was able to make out and touch the metal cluster on the man's shoulder. "Colonel Moore," he said grimly.

As he stepped out of the tent, exhaustion poured over him in giant waves. In his bewilderment he stared about like one pitchforked into a different world. The cries of orders screamed all about him. Lieutenant Walker Decklin could see the Confederates crashing through the Union lines at the end of the camping grounds. The hard, sharp sound of gunfire was all around him. Turning his head, he saw seven Confederates on horseback bearing down on him. Lead whizzed by his ear and spat into the ground beside him. He brought up his gun; it roared in his ear, and he heard a sharp cry and saw a trooper fall from his horse. Suddenly the force of a giant sledge hammer slammed into his chest, and he heard the report of a rifle. . . .

It was odd. He could hear sounds, but he couldn't move. He caught footsteps and voices, felt himself carried into a tent . . . then he lost all sense of feeling and time.

He heard someone saying: "If it hadn't been for the lieutenant here . . . we'd have been wiped out for sure. Too bad he won't make it. Doc, you sure he won't pull through?"

He heard another voice: "The bullet nicked the arch of the aorta, thus forming an aneurysm; the outer tissue has formed a bulged sack, like a balloon ready to burst. . . ."

"Break it down, Doc," said the first voice, "so we can understand."

"Nicked heart. He can go at any minute." Lieutenant Walker Decklin heard the snapping of fingers clicking together, punctuating the doctor's sentence.

Decklin made a tremendous effort to rise from his cot. His feeble effort to form the words: "Major Mitchel . . . I . . . must see him . . ." came only as lip movement.

Then strong hands were holding him down and a

voice kept saying: "Take it easy, lad . . . take it easy. Exert yourself and you're dead."

By noon, his breathing became so labored he had to be kept propped up on the cot. Every Unionist, from majors on down to conscripts who managed to poke heads into his tent, treated him as a hero. His reaction was one of no concern.

Major Mitchel, alone and standing above him, looked down. "I'm not pressing charges against any of your past actions, Lieutenant . . . you saved quite a few Unionists this morning . . . I've torn up the report."

"It doesn't matter now, does it?"

"Your official record will be clear."

Decklin started to laugh, then a cough broke in his throat and he felt the trickle of blood come to his lips.

Major Mitchel shifted his weight to his good leg. "Hear about your friend?"

"Do I have one?"

"Must. He helped you escape on the stage."

"Oh, you mean Hib . . ."

"That's right. Hib Kinsman. He was arrested just after the attack."

Decklin began to push himself up on his elbows. "Did he get the gold map?"

"You best not move, Lieutenant," warned Mitchel, easing Decklin down on the cot. "No. But he murdered Colonel Moore."

Walker Decklin managed one word: "Impossible!"
The sound of his voice was a long, low groan.

"Why?" replied Mitchel. "He thought the colonel
had the map. And *he* sure wanted it bad enough."

Decklin closed his eyes. "Would you mind leaving
me . . ." he mumbled, "I'm getting tired . . ." He
had to think this out. If he only had hours, possibly
minutes to live . . .

Major Mitchel's voice was as the bracing north
wind coming blowing up a valley when the air is
heavy with decay.

"There's a woman outside," said the major. "The
one on the stage. Been waiting ever since she
heard . . ."

"Julie?" Decklin opened his eyes. A scheme began
hatching in his brain. "Send her in," he said in a
stronger voice.

Holding the tent flap open, Major Mitchel stepped
out and ushered the woman in.

Julie Booth stood there a moment, leaning against
the center tent pole listening for the major's footsteps
to fade. When they did, she hurried over to Decklin's
cot.

"Walk . . . you've heard about Hib? Isn't it terrible?" Her soiled and torn dress was the same as
when he'd last seen her. Only now her reddish hair
was brushed neatly in a bun at the base of her neck,
and her face cleaned. She worked a hand up to her
throat and tried to look coy. She even tried fluttering
her eyelashes.

It didn't work. Decklin said, "You're here for a

purpose, Julie. What is it? What side are you on—North or South? You've never said."

"You're going to die."

"You needn't remind me."

"I didn't mean it the way it sounded."

"Would there be another way to say it?"

"Walk," she said moving closer, "I could always remember you."

The man on the cot rose from his pillow, cocking his weight on bended elbows. He tilted his head at her. "Just what does your conniving mind want of me?"

Red blotches of embarrassment crept up her neck. The shallow muscles of her jaw tightened, drawing into ugly little knots. "Remember, Walk . . . you said you wanted to repay me sometime for what Hib and I did for you!" Her voice raised a little higher than she really wanted.

"Go on."

"We—ll, since they've got Hib . . ."

Decklin interrupted: "*You* don't think Hib had anything to do with killing the colonel, do you?"

The laxness in Julie's face did not change, she saw to that; but her lips went white, like a person who has received a stunning blow without warning, and who, in the first moments of shock, does not realize what has happened. So expressionless was her face, he thought she had not heard him.

"I couldn't believe it," he continued, releasing his weight from his elbows and letting his body ease down to the blankets. "It's all circumstantial evidence they're holding him on. He's a civilian . . . has never said what side he'd champion if he'd be forced into this war. . . ."

Julie finally found her voice. "Don't be silly. Hib was with me at the time they said . . . the . . . it happened. It's a ghastly mistake, that's all." She fluttered her eyelashes again and lowered her head. "But Walk . . ." she murmured, "you have to help him."

Walker Decklin took a deep breath. "I think I know what you want," he said looking directly up at her. "Go bring Major Mitchel in here to me. . . ."

Her face lit up. "You'll say *you* did it, Walk?"

"Get Mitchel in here before I change my mind."

"It's no more'n right," she said, swishing out of the tent.

Within seconds she had the major and a stoop-shouldered doctor in a blood-splattered tunic crowded in the tent.

"What's this all about?" inquired Mitchel.

"Get a paper and pen . . ." began Decklin, but a cough broke in his throat and the doctor immediately hovered over him, testing the lieutenant's heart with the stethoscope that dangled about his neck.

Lieutenant Decklin made a move to brush the instrument aside as he looked up at the major and continued: "Deathbed confessions hold up in court, don't they?" He shifted his shoulders deeper into the pillow, trying to move away from the probing stethoscope.

The doctor, with a head of hair that looked like a sunflower gone to seed, became more persistent with his examination. A frown crinkled his brow and he looked up at his patient, but he uttered no word and quickly dropped his gaze to his stethoscope when the major replied.

"A deathbed confession does not even have to be written. Only a witness must be present . . ."

"Good," murmured Decklin, the tightness within his chest feeling like a steel band biting into his flesh. Growing annoyed at the doctor's continued fussing about his bandage, he brought up his hand and pushed the silver instrument from his chest and said, "How about letting a man die in one piece, not poked to death!"

"Hurry, Walk . . . hurry and tell the major . . ." Julie's hands were clutched before her twisting an already ragged handkerchief.

"Tell me what?" Mitchel said mildly.

Decklin took his eyes off Julie and said, "I . . . I killed Colonel Moore."

Instantly, quietness smothered down about the tent, as if all oxygen had been drained from the air.

Mitchel's mustache twitched once as he gritted his teeth. His eyes pierced the lieutenant in a protest of unbelief. "You know what this means?"

"I do," Decklin said in a penetrating accent.

"This confession will hold in any court," continued the major. "It'll free Hib Kinsman. No matter how I hate to do it, I'll have to turn that devil loose." Major Mitchel gripped the tent pole until the tendons in his hands stood out like white cables. "You admit, then, that you're a traitor to your country?

You weren't moved by a single emotion except greed? You murdered Colonel Moore for the map? Was that map to be used for your own purposes, or the Confederacy? To be a spy for the enemy is inconceivable!" Mitchel's anger made his voice climb higher: "Lieutenant, don't you realize how many lives of Unionists *you* saved when *you* rode into this camp!"

Decklin's reply was a lowered head. "I have nothing further to say," he mumbled grimly. "If there's no paper for me to sign . . . then what I just said is it . . . no more, no less." When he lifted his eyes, he saw that Julie Booth was smiling.

Major Mitchel kept studying the man on the cot. He took another consideration of Decklin's tense face. The rawhide-taut hush was broken by his firm voice: "Lieutenant Walker Decklin, I don't know why you've confessed. But it's a lie!"

Looking up at the major, Decklin felt as if he was transparent. He tried to muster up enough false anger in his voice to sound irritated: "Sir . . . you've said yourself my confession will hold in court. Now, I would greatly appreciate it if you would leave me alone with Miss Booth . . . I'd like a few words with her. And when you release Hib Kinsman, send him to me."

The doctor cleared his throat and Decklin looked up to see glistening beads of sweat on the man's face. "I'd like a few words with you myself, Lieutenant," said the doctor softly.

"No need to," replied Decklin. "Just go and let me alone. Let's not get emotional about this thing . . ."

The doctor shrugged his shoulders and followed the major from the tent.

When they had gone, Decklin held out his hands, palms up, to Julie standing at the foot of his cot. "Satisfied?"

"Why not?"

"If I thought for an instant Hib did it . . ."

"Dead men don't think."

"You'll do anything to get your hands on that gold map. Even get this lie out of me. . . ."

"I didn't twist your arm. And it's no lie now. It's a deathbed confession." She laughed softly, a taunting laugh.

"Gold means that much to you."

"If you must know, I don't want it for myself."

"Who else?" His face began to get more color in it.

"We *are* fighting a war. Or have you forgotten?" She laughed again, and moved up the cot's side to leave the tent.

"You dirty little rebel!" He reached out and grabbed her arm, his fingers digging deep into her flesh. "Does Hib know of this?"

Her hand flashed out and smacked him across the cheek, hard. "I don't have to answer to you!" She jerked free of him. He fell back.

"You must be pleased with yourself, Julie." His left hand traced the smart on his cheek. "Since I'm gentleman enough, just yet, I won't slap you down as you deserve . . ." His words trailed off. "But you haven't gotten that map . . . and *you* won't . . .

I'd advise you to get out of my sight before I forget I am still a gentleman!"

"Is that a threat?"

"Call it a promise."

She laughed again. It sent a shuddering chill through him. "I always wanted to see a Unionist die, slow. But you . . . I wish you'd live to be shot as a traitor!" She grabbed at the tent flap, jerked it back and stepped outside.

Not long after she had left, the doctor came in. He stood there a moment, just inside the entrance, without saying a word. Just staring at the man on the cot. A blank look took over his wrinkled face. He took from his tunic pocket a pair of shallow gold-framed spectacles and put them on. They weren't on his face a second until he removed them and began wiping the glass on the soiled hem of his floppy tunic. Fidgeting them on again he mumbled under his breath and jerked them off, slammed them into his pocket and came closer to his patient.

Decklin said, "I'm the one dying. Why are you so nervous?"

The doctor tried to straighten his hunched shoulders, but couldn't. "There's another woman outside to see you." He sighed. "She's from the La-dies' Welfare Brigade that makes regular visits to the wounded . . ."

"And the dying," grimly interrupted Decklin.

The doctor ignored him. "The ladies bring the men home-cooked baskets of food." He started to fuss with his glasses again.

"That shouldn't make you so nervous." Decklin edged his shoulders up until he was half sitting. "If you're afraid I'll take some food from a patient that's not dying," he let a smirk touch his lips, "I'll refuse what she offers me."

The man's voice became velvet soft, yet there was a forced huskiness to its quality. It trembled now as he said, "Hasn't it occurred to you that *doctors* have been known to make mistakes?"

Decklin cocked his head to the side. "What are you trying to say?"

"Lieutenant . . . you are not going to die."

For an instant, Walker Decklin closed his eyes. The world was going round and round.

"Since you pulled through the night . . ." came the man's voice, snapping the lieutenant back to the present.

Decklin looked up, his voice piercing and reproachful as it penetrated every part of the tent: *"I'll live?"*

The doctor nodded his shaggy head. "Chances are all in your favor . . . if you take it easy. I made a terrible mistake . . ."

"My Lord . . . do you realize *how* terrible?"

"I take it you mean your confession? I don't blame you, if you hold me responsible. That man you had released must mean a great deal to you."

Decklin's fists were balled about the edge of the blanket. "I guess I did a pretty good job on my confession."

"The major was right. You did lie?"

Decklin nodded.

"I was afraid of that," muttered the doctor.

A thought struck Decklin and his hands loosened on the blanket. "Get Major Mitchel back here . . ."

"I don't think it'll do much good."

"Why?"

"I heard him giving orders to have Kinsman released. He'll have to hold someone . . . you're the most likely."

"Get Mitchel, anyway."

The doctor shuffled toward the tent flap. He turned. "What about the lady outside?"

A willowy, tall woman pushed aside the canvas and stepped inside the tent. "What about the lady?" she said, smiling down at Walker Decklin, a wicker basket of cloth-covered food in her arms.

Decklin's eyes widened. His face took on the shocked appearance of seeing a ghost. "Susan!"

CHAPTER SEVEN

He looked at her curiously. Her hair was almost mahogany-colored in the failing light; she stood straight and tall, with a quiet confidence that Decklin had noticed when he first set eyes on her seven years ago. She was small, and yet she wasn't. The pink voile dress plainly showed her matured figure. The white cotton shawl carelessly tossed over square shoulders and the food basket gave her a girlish, care-free appearance. But the solemn look on her face betrayed her years.

Looking up into her brown eyes, he saw a faint shadow of hurt in them. She moved closer, unwrapping the cloth from the basket; then he saw his mistake. This wasn't Susan MacKay.

"Aldis . . ." he said, softly. "I'm sorry. I thought you were Susan."

She handed him a tin container of warm chicken broth.

"You must have loved my sister very much, to still remember how she looked."

He lowered his head and refused the food. When he looked up, he mumbled, "Can you forgive me, Aldis? But you look so much like her."

87

"Because of that . . . I don't want your sympathy."

He could see she was hurt, no matter how she tried to conceal it. "Is that why you wouldn't see me any more? You thought Susan would always be between us? Is that the reason you never let me know where you were?"

She placed the basket on the floor. "Something along those lines."

"You startled me, Aldis. You do resemble her, you know. It was a shame she was killed. . . . Maybe she and Hib . . ."

Aldis widened her eyes and said grimly, "If it makes you feel better, Walk, Susan told me she loved Hib." She watched him grow uneasy and start to shift on the cot. "But you've been misinformed. Susan committed suicide . . ."

There was a quick roughness in his voice. "She *what?*"

"Susan found out Hib was living with another woman . . . and she was carrying his child . . ." Her head tilted scornfully. "You didn't know?"

"Hib said . . ."

"Oh, I can imagine what he told you," she interrupted, "and it's all lies, as usual!"

Decklin's fingers had grown cramped from clenching the blanket hem. "I think when Hib's time comes . . . he'll even lie himself into his grave."

"You've saved *his* life by a lie."

He glanced up. "You know?"

"I couldn't help hearing, when I was waiting outside. You are a brave and foolish man." She started to bend down toward him.

"I'm a fool." He looked up and saw her face inches from his, setting his pulses throbbing. "Aldis . . . if I get out of this mess . . . will you marry me?"

"Where'll we go?"

"Joel's getting himself started in the cattle business. I'm a pretty good veterinarian . . . we could tie in with him."

Her brown eyes sparkled as golden flakes caught in them from the last rays of the sun. "You're asking *me?* And not Susan?"

He cupped her chin in his hands and drew her face to his. She came down to the cot. They never quite knew how it was that they were suddenly embracing. "I'm only half a man," he whispered along her ear, "lookin' for the other half . . . you. Does that answer your question?"

They were in each other's arms when Major Mitchel burst into the tent, his campaign hat dangling in his fist. "What's this the doctor tells me?"

Aldis MacKay quickly rose and brushed the wrinkles from her dress, scarlet making its way up her throat to her face.

Mitchel looked at Walker Decklin. "You trying to say you *lied* when you made that confession?"

Decklin nodded.

Mitchel raised his white eyebrows. "That's because you've found out you aren't going to die, I take it!"

"No, it's the truth!"

"I don't know any truth! Because of you, Hib

Kinsman has been released. . . . How do I know he
wasn't the one—if you say you aren't. What am I to
believe?" His shaggy mustache twitched at every lip
movement; he looked like a man who would lock
horns with General Grant himself. "What makes a
man tell such a lie on his deathbed . . . to save a
scoundrel?"

"Many things—and yet nothing," replied Decklin.

Mitchel's clenched fists whitened. Words came to
his lips and died there, and for a space he just stared
into Walker Decklin's eyes. Finally he formed the
words carefully: "Now, I take it, you want me to forget all about your confession?"

"I didn't kill Colonel Moore. I confessed to his
murder when I thought I was dying, so that an innocent man might be saved."

"Hogwash! This Hib Kinsman has some hold over
you!" He spun on his heel and went to the tent entrance, calling: "Guard . . . Guard! Surround this
camp! Don't let that civilian Kinsman get out!" He
came back to the cot and said, "Your friend won't get
away."

"You have no proof *he* did it."

"*You* have none that he didn't," snapped the major.

"Give me a chance . . . I'll find him. If Hib gets
cornered, he won't come back under force."

"One way or the other, he'll come back. I want
him questioned."

"Sir, give me that chance to find him first."

"Why?"

"My life depends on it. I'm not guilty. If Hib Kinsman *is* guilty—as you believe—release me. I know I can bring him back and he can straighten up this whole mess."

"You'll hunt him down?"

"I'll bring him back."

"What if he admits he killed Colonel Moore? Will you still bring your friend back to be shot?"

Decklin lowered his eyes to the blankets.

"That hardly answers my question, Lieutenant."

Decklin's face turned empty of expression. "Try me."

"You think I should believe you, after you've lied in such a way that *no* man'll ever believe you again? Why, even if I could help prove your innocence of this killing and treason . . . even if I did, you would have at least twenty years of prison ahead of you for the worst kind of perjury on the face of this earth."

Aldis MacKay, white-faced and trembling, went to Decklin and put a hand on his shoulder.

Major Mitchel continued: "By all laws, Lieutenant, man-made and otherwise, you are guilty—if not of one thing, then of the other. I'm sorry, but that's the way the cards stack up. I truthfully cannot say if I'm glad you are going to live or not. I'm not playing a game!" He turned and went toward the entrance. "Lieutenant Decklin," he added in a very soft tone, "you will be placed under guard. I don't know when

I'll see you, but I assure you it'll be at your court-martial . . . I'm leaving Stillwater to join forces with General Banks at Sand Springs."

"What about the gold map?"

"I was wondering when you'd get around to that." Mitchel dug a cheroot out of his pocket, put it between his teeth and clamped it there. "You'd like it if I told you where that map is, wouldn't you? I'll say this much. It's safe and it's going to end this war . . ."

"I hope so."

Mitchel raised his eyebrows. "Don't fight a war with yourself, Lieutenant. You'll never win." Without another word, he stepped out of the tent.

Aldis reached down for the soup container on the sod floor. Handing it to Decklin, she said, "You must eat . . . conserve your strength."

"What for? Fatten the hog for slaughter?"

She turned from him, saw the bulky form of a trooper walk up to the tent and stand with his back to the flap. Then she was leaning over Walker Decklin, her voice coming in a faint whisper. "Do you think you could ride a horse, Walk?"

"What are you talking about?" He took a deep breath. His chest didn't hurt as much as it did last night. "I think so."

"They won't think it could be done so soon . . . won't expect it . . ."

"You mean . . . ?" His face grew brighter.

"Yes. I'm helping you to escape. I'll get the guard's attention . . ."

"How?"

Putting her hands on her hips and turning sideways, she smiled. "You're not a woman."

"I'll need a gun."

"Horse and gun will be over by the east end of camp, hid in the trees. It'll be up to you how you get past the men."

"My uniform over there," he nodded at it heaped over a box at the side of his cot, "should fool them." Then, looking down at the foot of his cot, he smiled when he saw the major's forgotten hat. "That will hide my face."

"Now remember . . . eat what you can. I'll leave the basket." She bent and kissed him. "I don't know when I'll see you again . . ." She smiled. "When I do," she brushed her fingers across his cheek, "I hope you have a shave."

"It shall be done," he replied, and happiness ran through him.

She said, "Good luck . . . and *Voya con Dios,*" her soft voice sounding like a hymn. Then she hurried from the tent.

CHAPTER EIGHT

The early evening was warm, rich with the scent of growing things, and a hint of coming rain. A young moon rode up into the sky and shone down on the figure that emerged from the rear of a tent.

It had taken Lieutenant Walker Decklin over an hour carefully and noiselessly to undo the canvas at the seam.

Mellow moon glitter lingered on Aldis talking to the guard at the front of the tent.

"Miss," came the guard's hushed voice, "you're not supposed to be here."

"Why not?" came her soft whispering laughter. "You're here. I saw you this afternoon and wanted to come . . ."

"Well, now . . . if that's how it is . . ."

For a fleeting second, Decklin felt the urge to dash up there and stop the mockery with a well-placed fist to the man's chin; but the bright night told him he must hurry. His stride was cautious as he glided from tent shadow to tent shadow, working his way to the cottonwoods.

He needn't have been too cautious, for troopers were dashing this way and that, paying attention to

nothing other than their own chores. He began
walking right among them with no trouble at all, his
blue uniform and campaign hat blending well with
the others.

Gaining the trees shadows, he stopped and leaned
against a red cedar to catch his breath.

Leaving the shadows, he moved forward. Sound of
the men making ready for battle caught his attention.
There in the silhouetted night he saw the Unionists
lining up in columns of fours, checking and re-
checking their guns, waiting for the cavalrymen to
finish their chores. For a moment he was entranced
by the sight of the 31st Division. These were
Mitchel's men making ready to join forces with General Banks at Sand Springs.

He lingered a short time longer, looking down at
the battery and supply wagons and ambulances that
were precisely aligned to the last fraction of an inch.
Behind them were the caissons and, last of all, the
five bronze Napoleons. The Union soldiers, their flat
forage caps sitting cockily, their uniform coats but-
toned to the last button, dark blue and gleaming in
their cleanliness, awaited their commands.

Decklin rubbed a hand over his chest and was
glad the wound hadn't re-opened. He started forward, slowly moving up to the bay horse in the thickets. It nickered. Quickly he reached out his hand and
stifled any further sound from the bay by firmly
holding its nostrils for a moment. The swiftness of
his movement cut a sharp pain across his chest. He
reached for the rifle Aldis said would be in the scab-

bard, and shrugged when he couldn't find it. The scabbard was there all right, but it was empty. This wasn't like Aldis MacKay; something was wrong.

Cautiously he turned the bay to face downhill so that he could mount without too much effort. Making sure the cinch was tight enough, he started to put his foot in the stirrup, only to hear a voice from the shadows.

"If you don't mind, buddy, I've had my eye on that bay for a couple of hours. You'll have to get yourself another pony. Turn around easy-like, or this rifle I've got leveled on your backbone just might go off."

Decklin's heart skipped a beat. Slowly he turned, started to raise his hands; then he saw Hib Kinsman step out of the shadows, and he lowered his hands.

"Walk!" The surprise was greater in Hib's voice; he stepped closer, not letting his rifle lower a trifle. His face held the shifty look of the hunted; his white plantation suit was a dirty, mud-splattered gray. His voice came again, this time in a hoarse croak of amazement: "I thought you would be dead!"

"It was a mistake . . ." Decklin's anger surged to the surface. "As it was for me to have said what I did!"

"I'd have said the same for you, if I'd have been in your place."

"That true about Susan?"

Hib's jaws twitched. "Aldis has been talking to you." His knuckles on the rifle stock bunched into angry knots. "She's never liked me."

Decklin stepped forward, fists clenching.

"Keep back," warned Hib, his rifle never wavering.

Decklin stopped. "You don't care if I'd get court-martialed if it would mean getting your dirty hands on Mitchel's gold map. "Come back and explain to the major . . . come back with me so we both can prove we never killed Colonel Moore . . ."

"You might. But I can't."

"Then you did do it."

"I thought he had the map."

Decklin took another step toward Hib Kinsman.

"Don't try anything you'll be sorry for later," warned Hib.

"Hib . . . too late your conscience will stop you." He put his hand on the bay's shoulder. "Why don't you wise up?"

"Get away from that horse."

"I'm going to tell you something, and it'll only be once. You're coming back to Major Mitchel with me. You'll come back even if I have to whip you, and I will. I'll whip you so you'll scare your own pony when he sees you!"

Hib Kinsman pointed the rifle squarely at Decklin, and laughed. "Look, Walk, I got the rifle and you have the horse. Who do you think'll win?"

"Not you, Hib. Your winning days are dead."

A film of whiteness spread under the leather of Hib's face. "Ah, come off it, Walk. If it hadn't been for me, you'd be pushin' up daisies, back at the stage ambush."

"That's another thing. Why didn't those Apaches kill all of us?"

"Who do you think put 'em up to it? Gave 'em guns?"

"*You?*"

"Why, sure. It was the only way . . ."

"All this time you've been after the major's map. Not once have you given me a thought in your whole rotten scheme!"

"Okay . . . okay . . . have it your way," growled Hib. "You got tangled up in it . . . got in the way."

"The innocent men you let get killed . . ." whipped Decklin, and before the words were out of his mouth, he leaped forward, forgetting his wound.

Hib snapped his knee up in a feint at Decklin's crotch. Decklin twisted away and slammed his fist full into Hib's face. Hib Kinsman went to his knees and fell face down, the clumsy rifle extended above his head. Decklin jumped across him, for the rifle. He felt Hib twisting under him too late. An arm came down in hand-axing arc; the blow of the rabbit punch drove Decklin full length on the ground. He swerved away and smashed the edge of his fist into Hib's face.

The moment was brief and savage. Then Hib was pulling himself to his feet, grabbing the rifle by the barrel and swinging it.

Decklin felt a dull explosion of pain in his right shoulder as the rifle stock connected. He tried to raise his fist, but his arm was dead of feeling. He saw the rifle club rise again and got his shoulder into Hib's

wet, bleeding face and crowded Hib Kinsman back
against the horse. The rifle struck above his kidneys.
He cried out, and the gaunt, rocky face before him
smiled; the deep-socketed eyes, dull as stone, watched
him slip down.

Decklin struggled up, gasping. Hib let him gain
his feet and sway before him.

"I told you, Walk," he said, "you or nobody'll stop
me from getting that map. You know I mean it now."

Decklin could hear nothing now, but a great
roaring. Then that engulfed him. . . .

CHAPTER NINE

The velvety darkness of the sky was bright with stars. The valley of Sand Springs was a dull bed of silver under the night. And out of it came the soft laughing rustle of wind-stirred grasses, while in the sky from rim to rim the fat stars glittered down on Mitchel's 31st Division as they drew closer to the objective with General Banks.

But swiftly the distant billowings of the forests about Sand Springs were changing their tones and colors under the darkening approach of a storm.

Then the rain came, sweeping gusts that fell in great rolling veils of dimness. Scarcely had it struck in all its hissing force against the 31st tramping in the open, when a Confederate bugle blared out its brassy: *"Charge!"*

The woods surrounding Mitchel's Division, both front and rear, came alive with graycoats!

For a split second, Major Mitchel froze in his saddle. Then his command was quickly issued: "Second platoon!" His voice repeat going back through his linked files . . . an echo so fast it was like hail on a tin roof. "Posts!" The cannoneers took their stations by the pieces. "Action left!" Mitchel yelled at

the top of his lungs and the guns unlimbered quickly.
He called out again, his voice hoarse, his brain in
complete confusion. "Drop 'em right here." He flung
his arm to the spot where the guns were to be set up.
"Twenty-five-yard intervals. Hurry—load with canis-
ter!"

They reloaded, instead of standing with knife at
charge bayonets. Half-reloaded, the Confederates hit
them.

It was bloody clumsy. The Confederates had the
advantage of surprise, and their big guns from the
hidden slopes fired a volley as their mounted troopers
charged forward. Mitchel saw the Confederate guns
leap back in crashing recoil, then came three explo-
sions. That was when the mounted graycoats
swarmed forward; their horses' hoofs topped into
faces and chests. Then the charge broke and turned
in a thrashing mill to smash back through the
gouting shambles from the rear. The smoke cleared
and the unwounded Unionists tried firing at the enemy with rifles and finally succeeded in turning them
back. But the 31st had suffered a number of casual-
ties.

Then two Napoleons of Mitchel's Division roared
together in a deluge of whitish smoke. The rammer
staffs whirled, the rain beating down on their backs;
the No. 1 Napoleon rammers thrummed the vents and
fresh charges were rammed home.

Two more times the guns fired . . .

The second blast was short of its objective; the
Confederates turned their guns on the 31st and bom-

barbed them unmercifully—kept it up for half an
hour.

To the west and northeast, the mountains
trembled with man-made thunder and wild rebel
yells, then ceased as the remainder of Mitchel's broken, bloody men sought shelter in the neighboring
woods. They were cut off from their cannons . . . rifle and fixed bayonets were their only
weapons now.

The 31st knew they were surrounded . . . out-
numbered. Major Mitchell, standing his mount on a
slight rise, the mud swirling about his horse's hoofs,
gave another command: "Line up and charge . . ."

But a Confederate's rifle cracked, and Mitchel
toppled to the mud; his command was not carried
out.

All through the dripping night, Confederates and
Unionists waited for the other to make the first move.
It was three o'clock in the morning when the Con-
federates made their final rush.

Lieutenant Decklin urged his stolen chestnut
along the tracks of Hib Kinsman that fringed the
churned trail of the 31st.

Then the roar of distant cannon cut the morning
mist. He pulled up and tried to focus his eyes
through the haze. Drawing his arm across his eyes, he
looked down and saw where the hoofs of many horses
had joined the tracks of Hib Kinsman.

Without warning, he slammed heels into the chestnut's ribs and lunged ahead, the horse giving a surprised grunt.

The depressing sight of the battlefield rolled out before him, the veil of rain gently folding over stilled bodies of both men and horses.

Both graycoats and blue lay scattered where they had fallen during the night's battle. Seeing a Confederate boy, no more than sixteen, a peacock feather dripping from his campaign hat, Decklin pulled rein.

He looked down at the boy, sitting against a tree, scarlet spilling over his gray jacket. Decklin dismounted.

He found himself kneeling in the mud to touch a shoulder made knife-thin by hunger. The touch was all the boy needed— A reminder, however useless, that he had not been entirely forgotten.

The boy was smiling as death supplied its own belated anesthetic, and the body folded over the lieutenant's knees—to rest there a moment, then slip off and rest face down in the mud.

Lieutenant Decklin looked up, and saw the legs of the horses surrounding him. A voice came from the mist: "Colonel Viking, shall I shoot him?"

Decklin's hand flashed to his side—then he remembered he was unarmed.

"No," came another voice, and a rider moved closer.

Walker Decklin looked up and he could make out the form of a Confederate colonel sitting on a gray gelding. His jaws clenched until they hurt like no other pain he had ever experienced.

"Hib," was all Decklin could say.

Hib Kinsman laughed, the sound of it breaking on a high note. "Surprised?"

"Not any more." Decklin's voice was dry and dull. "It didn't take much doing to change your name to Viking!"

"*Colonel* . . . Colonel Viking, if you please," said Hib, the laughter dying from him. Turning to a trooper at his side, he muttered, "Take him prisoner, and be sure you tie him up good and tight . . . I don't want him getting loose."

Decklin felt himself sharply turned around, his wrists crossed behind him and jerked to his feet. "Get your map yet?"

"That's a worry to you, isn't it? That's why I want a talk with you. I sort of think you can tell me just where it is . . ."

Decklin interrupted. "Hib, which one of your names do you want me to carve on your headstone? Which name do you want men to remember you by? You don't have much choice, because you've ruined whatever name you've latched onto."

The colonel kneed his mount closer to the lieutenant, drew a foot from his stirrup and, without warning, slammed it into Decklin's chest, throwing the lieutenant to the mud.

"There's nothing in a name! It's the man behind it!"

Lieutenant Decklin got to his feet. "I see no man!"

Hib Kinsman wheeled his gray to the left with

such a vicious yank on the reins that the gelding let
out a squeal. "You'll know you've met one when I'm
finished with you." He nodded to his sergeant. "Take
him."

CHAPTER TEN

For two weeks, the seasonal spring rains of '65 had fallen steadily. Lieutenant Walker Decklin, confined to the prisoner stockade on the Missouri border, a wafer-thin-sided barn that housed 150 or more wounded Unionists, gained his strength rapidly.

Every day, Hib had questioned him concerning the gold map he was sure the lieutenant knew the whereabouts of. The colonel tried every device to make him talk—from beatings by the Holly twins to starvation.

"If you tell me," Hib once said gently, "I'll turn the prisoners loose."

Lieutenant Decklin had smiled. *"You* want me to believe that, *Colonel Hib Viking?"*

Hib had expelled his breath briskly. "I didn't think you would. . . . I could have Aldis MacKay picked up. *You'd* talk then, I bet."

"How'll I tell you something I don't know?"

Murder trembled in Lieutenant Walker Decklin as he thought of the past weeks. This was the first day Hib hadn't pulled him out of the barn to question him. He knew that only a smattering of the 2,000-

odd Confederates remained at camp since morning
. . . the others riding off with Colonel Viking.

It was evening, and he wasn't expecting the usual
treatment when the squeaky barn door opened and
blond Given Holly edged his bulk inside. His cold
gaze swept the lamplit room.

"Okay, bright boy," he growled, "move it outside."

Gills Holly was right beside his twin brother, bayonet fixed and holding a lantern in his other hand.
He grinned hopefully at seeing Decklin look down at
the rifle. "Don't tempt me to use it, Yank," he said,
and motioned Decklin out into the drizzling rain.

Given slammed the door, dropped the twelve-foot
log latch in place, and the twins herded Decklin
toward a shed at the side of the barn.

"Bring him over here where it's dry, Sergeant,"
called a woman's voice, "and leave us alone."

"Well, Miss, we'll be right in callin' distance," said
Given Holly, "if you find need to want us."

"That's right," chimed in Gills, and both men
gave Decklin a healthy shove. He slipped in the mud
and would have lost his footing if he hadn't grabbed
out at the four-by-four post.

Looking up, he saw the woman. "Julie," he gritted, "you dirty little liar," and made a rush for her.

"Think it over, Walk," she said, stepping back and
raising her hand slightly. Looking down at her hand,
he saw a pearl-handled derringer pointed directly at
his stomach.

"I guess *you* would pull the trigger."

"You know I would."

"We——ll, what do *you* want this time? It must be pretty good to get you out in the rain. If it has to do with that map, you're wasting your time." He started to turn back to the barn.

"No . . . don't go, Walk," she called, anxiety in her voice. "It's not that. It's Hib."

"Oh?" He turned around and began rubbing a hand along his beard-stubbled chin. "The *colonel* is drowning, and you want me to pour water on him?"

"He was wounded this afternoon, when they caught up with General Banks." Her face sobered more. "Not bad, but it's bothersome. I want you to see what you can do for him."

"He send you?"

"No."

He stared at her. "*You* stand there and ask *me* to help *Colonel Viking?*"

"Why not?"

"It would be a waste of effort and of time . . . that elusive, irrecoverable treasure, whose sands are as dust of diamonds . . ."

"Since your capture you have become *quite* poetic, Walk."

"Has there been anything else for me to do?"

"Then you'll come?"

"I just told you. I have *no* time for your Hib."

"You're a doctor."

"I'm a horse doctor. Your colonel is no better'n a mad dog."

She stepped closer. "You have to come."

"I don't *have t*o do nothin'," Decklin snapped,

pointing to the bruises his beard couldn't hide. "Do you think I did that to myself?"

Noisy movement at the barn door drew their attention. More prisoners were herded in. Decklin gritted his teeth.

She saw the concern on his face. "You're on the losing end of this war," she taunted, keeping her derringer pointed at him.

"That's your opinion!"

"Just who do you think those prisoners are? Hib . . . or I should say Colonel Viking, wiped out General Banks."

"You want me to believe that?"

"You don't have to. Just use your eyes."

He stared at her again. "And for that, you still think I'd help Hib?" He nodded at the gun in her hand. "Or do you think I'll do it because of that?"

He watched her tight lips form a thin smile, watched her drop the small gun in her handbag and come closer to him. "If *it* won't convince you, maybe this will." Her lips parted slightly and she swayed a little as she came to him. "Do it for me, Walk. Come help Hib, or he might bleed to death." Then she breathed on his throat: "I like a man in a uniform."

He thought about grabbing the handbag dangling at her wrist, for its derringer. Instead, he brought up his hands, placed them on her shoulders and gave her a push that sent her farther back in the skimpy shelter. "Well, let me stay in it!"

She stumbled against the cracked wood, her icy-blue eyes shining with the diamond brightness of frustration. "I hope you rot in that barn!" she screamed at him. "Hib'll see to it! I'll make him!"

Decklin stepped closer to her, backing her up against the wall. Her eyes swept wide with sudden fright, and she tried for the gun in her handbag, only to have him slam it to the mud with an angry thrust of his fist. His words came from deep within him. "You're nothing but a tramp. And I'm no gentleman!" He brought up his right hand and smacked her hard across the face . . . on one side . . . then on the other.

A sharp cry of pain came from her frightened lips. Both her hands went up to her face. "You beast!" she cried.

"I've got more where that came from. Do you want any more?"

"Hib'll kill you for that!" she whimpered, and watched him turn away into the shadows.

The Holly twins stepped from the barn and motioned him up to the latched door.

Julie began fumbling for her handbag in the mud. Finding it and jerking out her derringer, she leveled it at Walker Decklin's back. The report of the shot sounded like a giant firecracker. The bullet slammed into the four-by-four post beside Decklin's head, splinters of the slug spraying his face with stinging sharpness.

He spun on his heels to face her.

"See," she coolly called out to him, trying to smile, "I could have shot you . . . if I wanted."

The Holly twins leveled their rifles and backed away from him, giving her an open shot at him.

Walker Decklin looked at her. Not at the smoking gun in her hand, but at the woman's eyes behind that gun. He shrugged. "Well, Julie, why don't you?" He was stung by an absurd and maddening idea; he started pacing toward her. "Kill me now, Julie, and get it over with. Ever since I've known you, you've had that crazy desire to kill a man. Let it be me, and I'll be thankin' you."

The Holly twins had him by the arms before he had gotten any closer to the woman.

Julie lowered her gun. "You're a fool, Walk."

"Takes one to know one," replied Decklin.

CHAPTER ELEVEN

Inside the crowded building again, Lieutenant Walker Decklin noticed that the lamp had fluttered out, making the barn darker than the inside of a buffalo carcass. He pulled his damp jacket tighter about his shoulders as a chill cut him. Leaning back against the wall, he slid to the ground and began getting settled there for the night. Then someone called out to him, from the far side of the barn.

Wearily, he pushed himself up from the wet ground. "What is it?" He caught the form of a lieutenant bending over a man on the floor.

"Major Mitchel's near got his back shot off. He was brought in with the last bunch," came the reply. "See if you can do something for him."

Hearing the major's name, one all-absorbing thought took complete possession of his mind. Quickly stepping over inert forms and going around others that were sitting up, Decklin stopped beside Mitchel and folded at the waist, going to one knee. Momentarily he was stunned; the man's face he stared into belonged to Major Mitchel . . . but the clothes the major wore were the rags of a raw conscript.

112

"Get some light over here," Decklin mumbled.

"It's no use," muttered Mitchel. "Water . . . give me water . . ."

A dipper was passed through the darkness and Walker Decklin let the water trickle across the major's cracked lips and watched a stream of it trickle down the man's neck. He reached his hand across, and wiped the major's mouth with it.

"Thanks," murmured Mitchel, and opened his eyes. A strange blurry look came over him as he recognized Decklin. "How . . . how did you get here?"

"Take too long to tell."

"You're a prisoner?"

Decklin nodded. "Of Hib Kinsman's."

"I hear he's Colonel Viking? True?"

Decklin dropped his eyes. "I didn't know it until a couple of weeks ago." He raised his head and asked, "But why no uniform, sir?"

"Only way I could try to conceal my identity . . . but I'm sure your friend—Kinsman or Viking, or whatever his name is—knows I've been captured . . . that I still have the map."

"*You've* had it all the time?"

The major nodded, and Decklin could see the man was in pain. Suddenly he wanted the major to believe him. "If it'll mean anything to you, sir . . . I never killed Colonel Moore. But I'm afraid my lie cheated justice."

"It was this Kinsman, after all . . ."

"I didn't know it then, sir."

Mitchel turned his head slightly to the trooper

kneeling on the opposite side of him. "Do you mind, Lieutenant Hastings? This should be confidential."

"No, sir," Hastings said, and quickly faded among the other prisoners.

"Now get this," began Mitchel in a weakening voice. "I'll only say it once. I've been hard, but don't let it be said that I never gave a man a second chance when he needed it."

"What are you trying to say?"

"Lieutenant Walker Deckin, you made a deathbed confession and the real murderer of Colonel Moore went scot free. Don't you ever forget it—not in this world, or the next."

Within him, Lieutenant Walker Decklin felt the slow-growing inspiration of a new spirit. Mitchel believed him.

"Now, listen . . ." came Mitchel's harsh whisper, making Decklin lean closer to him. "I want you to do something for me."

"What makes you think I can?"

"You will . . . you'll have to. If not for one reason, then for the other. Your own, to prove your innocence."

"I thought you believed me."

"We—ll . . . I . . . I do. But there's the records. They'll have to be set straight."

Decklin grinned. Always the records with Mitchel. Even when he was dying, he thought about keeping regulations.

"I want *you* to escape . . ."

A laugh rose, then died in Decklin's throat. "I *want* to, too. We've tried it before . . . no go."

"You'll make it this time . . . because of this." Mitchel worked a hand beneath his bloody coat and brought out a sealed envelope. "Here's the gold map your friend wants so bad . . ."

"*You're* trusting *me* with it?"

"I have to. If any more know about it, I might just as well post its location on a bulletin board! Get the map down to General Sheridan . . . he's around Joplin . . ." A cough racked his body, and Decklin tried to raise his shoulders off the ground to ease him.

"Please . . . don't . . . just . . . just let me lie . . ."

"But sir," began Decklin, "how come you'll trust me with the map?"

Footsteps sounding outside the barn, hastily slopping in the mud, and coming closer and closer, made Mitchel quickly ease away from Decklin's knee and rest back on the ground. A fading whisper came from his lips. "Take the map, Lieutenant Decklin. Get it to Sheridan. At all costs . . . get it there. The envelope is sealed, and *must* remain that way. If the seal is broken, Sheridan will know the contents have been tampered with. Take it. If not for *my* reason . . . then for *your own*."

"But . . ."

"There's a note in it. It explains the mission of the bearer. Gawd, man, if I'm willing to trust *you* . . . take it!"

Just then, the barn door opened and a man holding a blazing lantern high above his head stepped in. The light flung its orange beam around the stable, catching Decklin's hand retrieving the envelope from Mitchel's heaving chest.

"I saw that," snapped Colonel Hib Viking, holding the lamp. "Bring it over here to me."

With cautionary movement, Decklin rose to his feet. He straightened his shoulders, his left hand clutching the sealed brownish envelope, and he saw the rifle cocked in Hib's right arm.

"Don't . . . don't give it to him," came Mitchel's tottering voice. "Don't do it. The Union needs all the gold . . they can get their hands on . . ."

"Bring it over," said Hib, reaching out his hand, and Decklin could make out the red blotch on the man's shoulder.

Looking down at the glassy-eyed Mitchel, Decklin gave him a glance of confidence and watched Mitchel's face suddenly relax with a frank smile. And in that moment, Lieutenant Walker Decklin knew he'd never see Major Mitchel alive again.

Making his way around and over the forms on the floor, Decklin was desperately making plans on how he could get past Hib. Getting closer to the Confederate, he asked, "Can we make a deal for the map?" and watched Hib's rifle level higher.

Decklin watched his words hit Hib like an ax.

"*You* want *me* to believe that?" Hib grumbled.

"I tried . . ." Decklin clutched the envelope at his side, stalling for time. "What brought you in here? You really didn't know Major Mitchel had this."

"Let's say this is my lucky day. Truthfully, Walk, I came in here to show you some manners, about how you treated Julie." It was simply said, but each word carried the certain promise of death.

Decklin took a step forward. "You won't shoot me," he said softly, tramping toward the entrance doors. "I'm leaving here . . . and you won't stop me Hib—not now, or ever . . ."

The confidence of the lieutenant dazed Hib into silence; he took one backward step. "Don't try it," he warned. "I'll kill you if I have to."

Decklin stopped. He was just an arm's length from the Confederate and knew he'd have to do something other than bluff. Slowly he straightened his tired shoulders; slightly crouching, he started to hand Hib the envelope.

When Hib made the mistake of reaching for it, with the hand that held the lantern, Decklin threw his body at Hib's middle, slamming him against the wall before he had time to bring up the rifle. With his right hand, Decklin axed down on Hib's neck and the Confederate went limp. The kerosene lantern dropped to the floor, bursting immediately to flames like a small explosion.

Forcing the letter into his belt, Lieutenant Walker Decklin tried to stamp out the spreading blaze in the dry straw.

"Forget it," called some prisoners. "It'll be our chance to get out of this pest hole!"

Decklin glanced down at the stunned Hib struggling to his feet and made a move to strike the man again. But he was stumbling toward the entrance. He looked to see if anybody was near . . . the guards were down at the far end under the overhanging roof. Decklin was stepping outside when a voice behind him called, "Walk . . . come back! Don't make me do it!"

Decklin leaped to the side. The deafening roar of a rifle filled the confusion of the barn, and the clubbing bullet slapped him hard against the back, throwing him out into the night on his knees.

The voice of Hib yelling, "Get that damned Yankee!" filled his ears.

Lieutenant Decklin felt a wave of sickening blackness begin to engulf him, yet he fought to a standing position, fell back against the barn wall to catch his wind, and saw the prisoners rush from the entrance. The whole barn was a sheet of flames, and the Confederates knew it would be wasted effort to try and quench the blaze. They stood and watched it while keeping the defeated prisoners under guard, dropping the ones who made tries for freedom.

Decklin managed his stumbling way to the overhang, where the Confederates kept their mounts, thinking there would be no guards about because of the excitement. Just as he gathered his strength to step to the nearest horse, a Confederate trooper ran down the other side of the shed, calling: "That you, Gills?"

Decklin's left hand reached beneath his jacket, reassuring himself he still had the map. Then, wincing against the flood of pain that washed through his body, he bent down and picked up a good-sized rock and called out in a gruff, disguised voice, "Over here . . . hurry up . . ."

Running feet found their way to Decklin's side of the shed. And as the form burst into view around the corner, the lieutenant rapped the Confederate on the side of the head with the rock. The man crumpled to a groaning heap.

Painfully reaching down for the Confederate's rifle, Decklin recognized the trooper as Given Holly. He smiled grimly and straightened with the bayoneted rifle in his left hand.

It took a few minutes to get one of the horses turned around.

He made the bare back of the horse in a vault of voiced pain, and hit unspurred heels to the chestnut in the same jump. Then, because the recklessness was wild within him, he headed straight past the blazing barn, taking the shortest path to freedom.

Guns winked out of the dark huddle of Confederates guarding the prisoners in front of the barn and bullets sang near him. Hooking his left leg against the chestnut's hip, Decklin leaned far down over the animal's neck and road Indian style on the "off" side of the horse until the barn was behind him, then headed for the vast darkness of the open range. He turned his face once toward the flames that were billowing upward, pushing the night back and bloodying the sky.

The chestnut was heaving when Decklin reined him up a rise of rain-soaked Missouri mud, and looked back. He saw the lights of the border town and blazing barn, flaming crimson against the darkened night. Then he saw a pencil line of cavalry hit the trail a mile behind him and suddenly knew Hib would do anything to get the map.

Wincing against the pain in his back, he pointed for the shadows of the tall trees, and openly cursed as the moon slid out from behind a cloud. Then intermittent lightning played over the valley's rim, threatening another storm, and shining down on the trail Lieutenant Decklin headed into. Rifle shots began hammering along his back-trail; the Confederates were still after him and shooting at shadows.

The moon rode over his shoulder as he loped on, and for a space of three miles the guns grew silent. Suddenly they opened up and he could hear the bullets sing past him. He lay low over the chestnut's shoulders and turned the animal down a brush-bordered draw, hoping to shake pursuit. A small herd of longhorns scattered as he rode in on them.

After he had followed the sandy bottom for nearly a mile, the Confederates slammed closer.

Then the lieutenant jumped a rangy cow browsing on the green leaves of the draw, with a calf too big to be following her, and he set upon them furiously, getting them to break into a full run, hoping they'd make enough noise so he could elude capture. At the next bend in the draw, Decklin turned quickly up the eastern bank and stopped in the brush, letting the cow and calf race ahead. He was glad to let the chestnut blow, and leaned down over the animal's neck trying to get his breath in painful gasps.

Quickly the knot of Confederates rushed by above him in a furious gallop, following the crashing of the cow and calf. He heard a voice yell out: "Don't let that damn Yankee get away," and recognized it as Hib's.

Hearing their hoofbeats fade in the night, he felt a drop of rain peck his cheek and cursed the weather. He kicked heels to the chestnut and plunged up the rocky side of the draw.

Reaching forward, he clasped a handful of mane, pulling his weight up off the animal's kidneys, enabling the chestnut a more sure-footed climb. By all accounts, he should have been safe, but the sweat-flecked chestnut hit a soft shoulder of mud. Instantly, Decklin pulled him around to face downhill to get his balance, but the sliding horse stumbled against a jagged rock and put a foreleg into a water filled gopher hole, upending in a somersault.

Lieutenant Decklin was thrown hard, with the wet ground coming up to slam his head and shoulders with stunning force. The fall cut a sharp cry out of him as the chestnut rolled heavily. The hip of the animal hit hard upon his right leg, crushing it against the protruding rock. Rolling down the hill, he dimly remembered seeing the horse rise, and, tail-up, take off at a full gallop.

Reaching the bottom, everything went hazy and the ground-shaking roar of the returning Confederates thundered in his ears, like a herd of approaching buffalo.

He knew enough to crawl into the shadowing brush before blacking out. . . .

CHAPTER TWELVE

When full consciousness returned to him, the thunderstorm had moved northward, dissipating its fury along the mountain ridges. Blood crept stickily down Decklin's cheek from a gash over his temple, and the concussion left a dull ache pounding in his brain. He rolled over. The sky was getting lighter; there would be another hour of thick half-darkness.

Not hearing any movement of the Confederates, he crawled back to the spot where the chestnut had fallen and found his rifle. Frantically he reached for the envelope beneath his muddy tunic. He breathed a sigh of relief when his fingers touched it.

The wound on his back proved to be a dull, aching throb, nothing other than a flesh wound, but it made him light-headed and rendered his right arm useless.

Lying in the mud at the bottom of the draw, he reached his left hand up to his right shoulder. Satisfied that his collarbone wasn't broken, he winced at the sharp pain when his fingers contacted the hard lump that told him the bullet was lodged against a muscle. He knew it had to come out. But how?

He shook his head, trying to clear his fogged thoughts, trying to cinch on to his bearings. Again he listened for the Confederates.

Satisfied the graycoats had gone, he used his rifle as a crutch and pulled himself to his knees with a moan and rose to his feet. The motion collapsed his right leg when he put his weight on it. Crumpling to the ground, he scraped his right arm on the bayonet. Before he gave further thought to his leg or predicament, he angrily jerked off the sharp blade and tossed it into the brush with a curse.

For a while he sat in the mud massaging his leg with his good hand, assuring himself that it wasn't broken—just twisted. He rose again, this time with all his weight on his left leg, leaning hard on his rifle crutch. His clothes were soaked; he felt miserable and chilled to the bone. Nausea racked his body and he wondered if getting the map to General Sheridan was worth it. But if Mitchel was man enough to trust him with the map, he thought, then he could be man enough to keep going.

But the tormenting prick of temptation touched his brain. A man's halo could become *too* tight. Just a fraction of that gold would put Joel, him, and Aldis on easy street the rest of their lives.

A crashing noise farther down the darkened draw halted his thoughts; his captors were returning. Spreading his legs apart to keep his balance, he raised the rifle and waited.

Lieutenant Walker Decklin knew he had it within his power to become a rich man—and a traitor. He remembered Major Mitchel's words: *"A man's conscience is his fort . . . he alone makes a Hell out of it."* Decklin half-laughed. "Fort Hell. I wonder how many men have died there?"

He pierced the misty dawn darkness with thready eyes, and swore he saw the brush to the left of the draw move. The Confederates had him surrounded; the noise crept closer. His face grayed. His shoulder wouldn't hold the use of his rifle; quickly he lowered it to his left hip, pressed the butt of it there with his elbow. His left hand groped for the trigger guard, then .

The crashing broke through the clearing with the bawling cry of a cow hunting its lost calf, and Decklin sheepishly lowered his rifle; had he pulled the trigger, the sound would have signaled his location.

Hobbling painfully up the side of the draw, he fell in the glass-slippery mud. Gaining his balance, he grabbed a bush and pulled himself up and over the edge. Lying there a moment, getting his breath in gasps, he heard the faint command, "Keep searching men; he's 'round here . . . he can't travel far," and recognized Hib's voice.

Now, as Decklin strained his ears in the murky dawn, he could hear the troopers spreading out, searching toward the northeast. He hobbled among the brush of the draw heading south.

Finally he became aware of his increasing fatigue, aggravated by the fact that he had nothing to eat since yesterday's dinner—if you could call turnip soup and hardtack food. He crossed a swift brook and found himself in hilly ground where dogwood buds showed a misty pink. His legs began to ache and the slop-slop of his sodden clothes sent little chills running through him.

Then, in the direction from which he had come,

he caught the echo of shots and was sure that he could hear angry voices. He wormed his way along the edge of the ravine, feeling for the brink with each step. Suddenly from out of the gloom and over the beat of his heart he listened and heard the weird throbbing bay of hounds.

Stumbling forward, careful of where he placed each foot, he saw the swift whitecaps of the water far below and caught the beat of the waves of the Osage River. For a moment, he studied the deep chasm of the ravine. If he could get down to the river, cross it, he could be on the Joplin side.

Whatever he decided to do with the map, he knew he had to shake the hounds.

Just as he was making ready to crawl down the steep side, a horse crashed the low brush on the trail and disappeared into the gray shadows. Crouching beside a clump of hanging willows, Decklin put his weight on his good leg, laid the rifle against his knee and tucked his useless right arm in his belt to keep it from dangling. Then he jammed the rifle stock against his left side. Chances were, he told himself, this was one of Hib's raw recruits; whoever it was was making too much noise for a seasoned tracker.

Then the sound of carriage wheels cut into the hoofbeats. For a scant second, the noise bewildered him. Scrubby willows and brush hid him from view until the horse and carriage were only an arm's length away. Instantly he stumbled onto the trail, wincing at the pain in his leg, and saw the dark form of a light barouche behind the nervous horse. The animal reared in fright as he grabbed for the reins.

"Take it easy!" Decklin croaked to the driver. "I won't hurt you," and saw he was talking to a big wall-eyed Negro sitting on the driver's seat.

Then he saw Julie Booth's angry face poking out from the rear section of the carriage, a small whip in her hand.

CHAPTER THIRTEEN

"Walk!" Julie gasped in disbelief, then quickly controlled herself. "Hib told me you escaped. Told me you have the map. You're crazy to think you'll reach Sheridan with it!" She grinned, a slow, lazy grin that exposed teeth as white as the pearl handle of the derringer she started to bring out of her handbag.

"Don't try that again," Decklin warned. He reached into the carriage and jerked the bag from her and threw it down the hill.

"Just what is *your* reason for wanting the map?" She spat the words. "Is it for the Union? Or just to prove your own innocence?" She began raising the small whip. "Or is it neither?"

He reached up and pulled the whip from her hand with a twist.

He watched contempt flood her eyes. "Walk . . . what makes you think you got a chance to get away from Hib?"

He said very casually, "My conscience."

She laughed. "You want me to believe *you'll* deliver that map to Sheridan?" Throwing back her head, she laughed again. "No man with that amount of gold within his reach would do it. *No man.* You

hear, Walk? No man has *that* kind of a stupid conscience!"

Decklin's eyes fixed on her face. "My mind is made
up," he said, shifting his weight.

She stopped laughing now. "What, may I ask,
made it up for you?"

He said very calmly, "You just did."

She could see that he was in a great deal of pain;
the least bit of physical effort would knock him off
his feet. Suddenly she was flinging a carriage blanket
at Decklin. He ducked its smothering bulk and
slammed his weight down on his bad leg. He
stumbled and went to his knees in the mud.

She was screaming to the Negro driver, "Get his
rifle! Get his rifle!" while she flung herself after the
blanket and jumped on Decklin like a clawing
mountain lion.

Lieutenant Decklin flung off the blanket and
slammed her back to the mud in one long sweep of
his arm. He watched her slip and fall at his feet, the
mud quickly soaking into her clothes as she fought,
squirmed, and screamed.

Decklin looked up at the scared Negro. "Stay right
where you're at, and you won't get hurt. You hear?"
He pointed his rifle directly at him.

"Yes sah," replied the driver, and sat riveted to the
seat.

Decklin spun the rifle on Julie as she scrambled to
her feet, smiling as she slipped, fell again and then
pulled herself up. Her thin lips pulled back in crafty
spite.

"Makes you feel important to strike a lady," she snapped.

"What lady? Some have to work at it longer." He watched her eyes slit. "Now get back in there, and get this buggy moving."

"*You're* leaving us?" Surprise was full in her voice.

"You, Julie, are getting me through Hib's lines."

"You're insane! Hib'll have us stopped before we get a mile from here."

He pushed her into the buggy and followed. "This says we'll get through." He patted the rifle. "Or you and your precious Hib won't see another Missouri sunrise. It'll be up to you." He couldn't help the groan that escaped him as he eased his body into a cramped position on the floor. He settled his aching bulk against her knees and tried to stretch out. Now toss that blanket over your lap and legs, and my back," he said, "and be sure you keep me hid with it."

She looked down into his fatigued eyes that were bright with defiance and knew he was angry and hurt enough to go through with his threat. "Walk," she cooed, "you're hurt. Why kill yourself for the Union? You and I, Walk . . . you and I could . . ."

"All right, Julie," he said disgustedly, pushing her hand off his shoulder, "I don't want to go through that again. Get this buggy movin'." He felt her stiffen and saw her nod to the driver. The buggy jerked forward and he pulled the blanket over his head.

It was quiet again, except for the sucking sound of

the mare's hoofs in the mud and the slush of the carriage wheels slapping against the uneven ground as they pressed forward into the murky dawn.

He knew he had to have his wound tended to, but he couldn't afford to have Julie do it . . . If he only knew where Aldis lived.

Finally the Negro called back, "Confederate boys comin' dis way, Miss Julie."

Lieutenant Decklin poked his head out from under the blanket. "Keep going until they stop you." He watched Julie's amused eyes ice over, and he gritted, "If you so much as hint you saw me, I'll shoot you first. I'm not foolin', Julie!"

Pulling the blanket over his back again, he felt her tuck it about her legs and down over his head. That was her answer. Then he heard the pound of hoofbeats and slapping clink of saber steel come closer and closer.

He felt the carriage stop and wait, then heard the Confederates pull to a halt, and judged there to be three or four horses. Then a voice called out, "Why, Miss Julie! You shouldn't be traveling by yourself."

Decklin stiffened, waiting for her reply.

"I'm not," she said. "I . . . I have Colin, my driver, with me."

The trooper laughed. "Have you see a Union lieutenant around?"

"You mean Walker Decklin?"

"Why—why, yes, that's his name, Miss Julie." The man was perplexed. "How did you know?"

"Colonel Viking told me all about him before I

left," she said, and felt Decklin relax. "No, I haven't seen a man on the trail. We did run into a polecat, though . . ."

The trooper laughed. "Isn't it somethin' 'bout us chasin' those blue-bellies outa Joplin?"

"You did? Wonderful!"

Decklin gritted his teeth. If the Confederates had taken over Joplin, where would he find General Sheridan? Then he heard the Confederate bid farewell and heard the hoofbeats fade into the distance.

Tugging the blanket off his back, he glared up at her, realizing how dangerously narrow his margin of escape had been. Sharpening his voice, he said, "You cut the deck thin that time . . . too thin, Julie," and started to pull himself up to the seat. He found the effort taxing his strength and saw that she was grinning at him.

He pulled himself up onto the seat. Beads of sweat glistened on his muddy face. Then he strained his voice up to the Negro: "Get out and unhitch the horse."

"Yes, sah," mumbled the frightened driver, hopping down.

"You don't really think you'll make good your escape?" Julie drawled.

"I can try," he said, leaning his head back and momentarily closing his eyes.

Julie's hand whipped out and grabbed for the rifle on Decklin's lap. Instantly he snapped open his eyes and flung himself at her, wincing at the pain it caused. He jerked the rifle out of her hands as he pinned her struggling form against the seat with his body. "Don't make me do something we'll both be sorry for later."

"I'll kill you," she whipped in his face, her breath fire hot. "I'll never let you get that map to Sheridan. . . . I won't . . . I won't," she screamed at him.

"What's the matter, Julie?" he asked softly. "Now tell the truth. I know it's hard for you—but try. Do you really want this map for the Confederacy or for yourself? You and Hib are both from the same greedy no-account, riffraff mold. My guess is that you'd kill one another for it." He patted his jacket front, showing her he still had the map. "You'll have to go some to get it off me." He pushed himself from her squirming body, only to have her small, clenched fist pound at his wounded shoulder.

Already he had been swept by a wave that seemed to lift all the weight from his body. He had set his teeth and fought it back. Now it poured over him again, like hot water, took him off his feet and seemed to toss him high above a tip-tilted world.

Forcing all his strength to the surface, he drew back his left hand and slapped her across both sides of her face. The sound of the blows snapped in the icy morning air like twigs cracking. "You Confederate she-devil!"

"I promise you, I'll kill you for that!"

"You told me that before, my little Confederate." His voice was husky. "Now get out of this carriage."

She stumbled to the ground and saw that the driver had the horse unhitched and ready.

"What foolishness do you intend now?" She turned and watched the trouble he was having climbing down from the carriage.

"This buggy won't get through the trail where I want to go." He leaned heavily against the running-board, all his weight on his good leg. Pointing the rifle at the Negro, he said, "Bring that mare over here."

Standing on the running-board, he had easier mounting. Still, it washed his body with pain, and he slumped forward.

"You won't stay on that horse five minutes," she warned, brushing back her hair with a fussy hand, "and you know you won't."

He straightened on the mare, took a deep breath, worked the rifle across his lap, and looked directly at her. "Get up behind me."

She took a step back. "I *most* certainly will not!"

He looked over at the driver. "Lift her up here." He watched the Negro stare blankly at him; he pointed the rifle at the driver's broad chest and spoke with more firmness: "I'm not playin' games."

Decklin saw Julie start to protest, then straighten to ramrod stiffness and let herself be lifted up behind him, her full dress and cloak flouncing down on both sides of the gray mare as she straddled the bare-backed mount.

Decklin turned to the Negro. "Now you take off for those hills"—he nodded to the north—"and don't let me catch you tryin' to contact any Confederates!"

"Yes, sah—no, sah," stammered the man as he began running for the shadows.

Picking up the short reins, Lieutenant Walker Decklin touched heels to the gray and started forward, heading in the opposite direction the driver had taken.

"Where are you taking me?" whined Julie.

"Since you know so much about everything—does Aldis MacKay live in these parts?"

"She does. But *I'll* not tell you where." She smiled a half-crooked grin. "Hib sent some men out after her."

"What?"

"Sure. Hib thought you'd tell him about the map if he had her."

"Did he find her?"

She laughed. "Did you tell about the map?"

They rode in silence for the next half hour as he pointed for the rocky hills. Once there, the hills on either side stood fast, uncompromising, clear-set in the atmosphere. Julie could feel the weight of him getting heavier and heavier against her.

The early morning air was clear and cold; the extreme sharpness of it acted on Lieutenant Decklin's nerves like an astringent, and the well-chain iciness of it chilled his damp uniform against his body until he began to shiver.

The woods were misty with low-lying fog as he pressed the gray forward under the trees and up the high climb of the hill. Easing down the slope on the other side, the Osage River roared and raced below them like a savage guide; across the water lay Joplin.

She laughed in his ear. "Now I know you're insane. You heard that we've taken Jolpin. Ride in there and you're a dead man."

He kneed the mare toward the noise of the river; he had to heel the mare hard to get her into the swirling water. "Hold tight," he said to the woman clinging to him, "if you don't want to drown."

She screamed in his ear, "Walk, *I can't swim!*"

He laughed at her, but the laugh quickly sobered in him as he watched the water slipping away from the mare's feet like a glassy floor of marble, green with veins of dirty white, made by the scum that was foam.

The mare began to flounder; he gave her a loose rein. The water came up to their waists; Julie clung to him, wrapping her arms about him.

"Sit still," he told her; and the mare began to swim easily and they made it safely to the other side.

The forest he headed into smelled of growing things after last night's rain; a few robins and orioles started to sing and flit about. He pulled rein on the rim of a rise and cocked his head to the side . . . listening . . . wondering if he had actually heard the fragment of hoofbeats.

Squinting his eyes through the misty fog, toward the east and at the bottom of the rise, he saw galloping along at the base of the hill four hundred feet below, a troop of thirty-six Confederates.

"That's Hib," cried Julie. "He's crossed the river.

A mile away, I can tell how that man rides! Still think *you'll* make it to Sheridan?"

The lieutenant turned slightly to face her. "One word out of you and I swear I'll drop Hib soon as he gets in range." He felt her stiffen behind him. "I mean it."

Holding tight rein on the mare, he hoped the animal wouldn't whinny to the other horses. He knew he couldn't dismount and hold his hand over her muzzle, for he'd never be able to mount again.

Without warning, Julie started to scream at the top of her lungs. He spun around and tried to clamp a hand over her mouth. She bit him. "Shut up," he growled, and felt his body go a little off balance.

Julie felt that sway of his body, and that was all she needed. She snapped her frantic gaze below, saw that Hib had pulled the men to a halt and was looking up. She screamed again and flung all her weight at Decklin, punching him on his wounded shoulder until he lost his hold on her.

Lieutenant Walker Decklin slipped to the ground. He tried to turn and grab for the reins, but she put a foot out and shoved him away, and slammed heels to the mare's sides.

As the horse jumped ahead, the shoulder of it struck the lieutenant in the chest and knocked him toppling down the hill.

"Hib," Julie kept screaming as she spurred the mare. "Hib . . . Hib, he's up here!"

CHAPTER FOURTEEN

Lieutenant Decklin was thankful that the muddy ground had somewhat cushioned his fall, but he had lost his rifle. Clattering clamor of the approaching cavalry thundered closer above him. He scrambled to his feet, grabbing for the envelope beneath his jacket. It was gone; lost in the fall!

At first, he did not think that the map meant victory to the Union. His first thought was—he had lost his chance at a fortune!

He looked up at the tree-lined ridge. There in the broken grass of his tumble lay the envelope and his rifle, in clear sight of anybody looking over the rim.

He could hear the Confederates coming up the hill at a full gallop, hear Hib's voice urging them on. "Spread out, men. I want that letter he's carrying, and I don't care how you get it! Just get it!"

Scrambling to the rim, Decklin managed to grab his rifle and crouch behind a cedar, just as Hib and the Confederates pulled in their mounts.

Hib's voice snapped: "Lieutenant Holly, take the men down the hill and don't come back until you have that Yankee! You hear?"

"Yes, sir," came the reply.

And in a crashing effort the men began their

search, while Lieutenant Walker Decklin backed farther into the shadows, his hand gripping the rifle, his
eyes fixed on the envelope in the mud—a full twenty
feet from him now.

He watched Hib dismount, and he hobbled to
another scrub-based tree trunk; he cursed when Hib
tossed Julie the reins and started down the hill on
foot.

Hib was only a few feet from stepping on the envelope, when Decklin reached down for a rock, smiled,
aimed it down the hill and threw, hoping it would
distract Hib from looking down and seeing the envelope. It did, for Hib called out, "He's down there
. . . don't let him get away." Hib took a few paces
forward and stopped.

Decklin held his breath as he watched Hib's boot
crunch down on the envelope and push it into the
mud and grass.

Standing on the envelope, Hib called up to Julie;
"Can you see anything from up there?"

"Only shadows," came her anxious reply.

"Well, he's around here, and I want him!" Hib
raised his voice and called to his men, "Keep spread
out!"

Hib never gave it a thought that Decklin would be
hiding close to the rim. "Ah, hell," he muttered,
"he's not up here," and turned to work his way back
to the horses.

With Hib's back to him, Decklin edged from the
shadows and reached down for the letter, snatched it
from the mud, and slid back to the underbrush.

"Hib," came Julie's frightened voice, "I saw something move behind you."

Hib spun and drew his .36 single-action, six-shot Whitney Navy Colt. "Where?"

"To the left."

Hib was quiet a moment, then said, "I don't see anything."

"Well, hurry up here . . . I don't want to be left alone."

Hib began climbing.

Decklin could hear the Confederates cursing and grumbling at the base of the hill, quirting their horses and forcing the animals into the underbrush with vicious jabs of spurs. He tucked the envelope into his belt, got down on his hands and knees and began crawling up to where Hib and Julie were talking beside the horses.

His back and shoulder were a burning ache; his right leg nearly made him cry out every time the swollen knee dragged over a rock. Clutching the rifle, he headed slightly to the left, hoping to come up behind Hib and Julie. Slowly he crawled to a clump of white flowering dogwood and just as he gained its shadowing arms of undergrowth he caught a glimpse of Hib looking over the edge; he could have sworn the man looked directly at him. Sweat glistened on his face, and he pressed closer to the muddy ground and held his breath.

"Did you hear something, Hib?" came Julie's voice, and Decklin saw her step closer to the Confederate.

"You got me believing I'm seeing things now
. . . I thought I saw something move."

"Where?"

"Down there by that clump of straggly white flowers."

"That dogwood?" She pointed out the bush where
Decklin was hiding.

"Is that what you call it?"

"Yes. But I don't see anything."

"Stand back," muttered Hib. "I'll send a shot into
it."

Lieutenant Decklin pressed his body closer to the
ground, trying to force his backbone through his
stomach and praying Hib's shot wouldn't find him.
He clutched the rifle at his left side, not making a
move to use it. Then as he glared up through the
compact purple-blotched young green leaves of the
dogwood, he froze in terror. Not from the Confederate
pointing his cocked gun in his direction, but from
seeing the slithering copperhead snake, worming its
way toward him!

The brown and copper pattern of the treacherous
skin melted into the background of mud and leaves;
Decklin had seen it too late. He knew if he didn't
attract the copperhead's attention, it might glide on
about its own way. But Lieutenant Decklin's nerves
were already rubbed too raw; he pushed himself
from the ground with a heave . . . away from the
oncoming snake, with no thought of Hib's cocked
gun.

At Decklin's sudden movement, the copperhead

created a buzzing sound by the vibration of its tail along the leaves. Its triangular head lunged forward, fangs extended; then a shot from Hib's gun sprayed Decklin's face with mud and he saw the coppery-tinted reptile slip out into the open, frightened by the splash of the bullet that hit the ground two feet between Walker Decklin's head and that of the snake's. Decklin was momentarily stunned; if he hadn't jumped back from the copperhead when he did, Hib's bullet would have been the end of him. As he watched the yellow-banded snake wriggle down the hill, he heard Julie laugh, "Hib, it was only a snake. See it crawl away? You're jumpier than I am."

"I could have sworn I saw Walk in that clump of bushes," came the still-undecided voice of Hib.

"Well, you were wrong."

Then a concerned voice at the foot of the hill called up, "Is anything the matter, Colonel?"

"Thought I saw the prisoner, that's all. Forget it, and keep looking," called back Hib.

Faint mutters of annoyance from the Confederates came up to Decklin, and he looked over to where he had last seen Hib. The man had disappeared.

Worming his way closer to the top, he pulled his body up to the cedar and rested a second. Then he heard a voice behind him snap, "Let's string out, men, and ride slow-like up the hill. That Yankee has to be around!"

Decklin had only seconds to get to the top, and surprise Hib. He pulled down a cedar bough with his numbed right hand, and let the spring of the branch drag him to his feet. Hib was standing beside his mount ten feet from him, his back to him, his arm about Julie's waist.

Without warning, Lieutenant Walker Decklin stepped into the open, leveling the rifle at Hib's back, and let go the cedar branch. The creaking crunch of the foliage spun the Confederate and the woman around. And Hib looked angrily into the black barrel of Decklin's hip-leveled rifle.

For a breathless moment, the two men stared into the eternity of each other's eyes. Hib could see Decklin's knuckles on his left hand grow white against the pulling trigger strain; his own hand hovered over his Whitney Navy Colt like a spread tan spider. He crouched.

"You planning something?" Decklin asked.

"No, just pointin' out where my gun is at," Hib quipped, moving his fingers from the holster.

Julie's voice rasped, "Walk . . . if you shoot Hib, his men'll cut you down before you take a step!"

Decklin could hear the Confederates urging their mounts around the steep incline behind him; he could feel the weakness start it's creep over him again.

"I'll drop one of you when I'm hit, the other when I'm on the ground. Think about it," Decklin said, and caught Julie out of the side of his vision taking a backward step toward the rifle hanging from Hib's saddle. "You're signing Hib's death warrant!" he said flatly.

"I don't think *you'll* shoot Hib." Julie watched her words strike Decklin with their bluntness.

Quickly she snatched for the rifle scabbard. "I'll get that map off you if Hib won't!" But before she cleared the rifle from its leather housing, Hib's strong arms twisted her from the horse.

"You wanting to get me killed? You little hellcat! Don't you know he'll do what he says!" Hib swung her around and pushed her viciously from the horse.

For that split second when she stumbled backward, Julie was speechless with anger. Then, like the flash of a snapping whip, her right hand flung out and connected with a resounding smack across Hib's face. "You're afraid of Walk!" she yelled. "You're scared silly!"

"Right now, Walk holds top card." Hib's words were filled with anger and embarrassment; his hand went up to his cheek.

"All right," came Decklin's husky voice, "bring those horses over here."

At first, they were reluctant to heed his order, but one look at the determination written on Lieutenant Decklin's unsmiling face made them do as they were told.

Decklin could hear the grunts of the Confederates' straining horses scrambling up the hill. "Soon as they reach the top, tell 'em to forget about looking for me."

"You're crazy as a hoot owl," said Hib."

"Maybe. But tell 'em to head back where they come from. And tell 'em you and Julie will follow later."

"They won't believe me!"

"Make them!" snapped Decklin, motioning with his rifle.

"They'll know something is the matter," whined Julie.

"It'll be up to you two to see they don't."

Without further comment, Hib pulled Julie over to him, glaring his silent annoyance at her, and jerked both their mounts beside them. Decklin pressed back into the shadowy growth with a last warning: "Remember, just get rid of them. I don't care how you do it—just be sure you do. I'll be right behind you." Then, seeing Hib trying to maneuver the horses between him and the cedar tree, Decklin quickly added, "Get those horses to the other side, Hib! I'm not foolin', and *you* know it! And remember, this rifle is pointed at you all the time. Now *move!*"

Hib muttered something incoherent, but pulled the chestnut and gray from the cedar. He no sooner had this done, when a pipe-smoking, beefy sergeant and six other troopers lunged their mounts up and over the rise. Pulling their heaving horses to a halt twenty feet in front of Hib and the girl, the burly sergeant clamped his teeth down on his smoldering pipe. "He flew the coop, sir."

"That's just what I'm beginning to think," Hib replied, and snapped his eyes at Julie.

Within minutes, the whole troop was restraining their mounts on top of the rise. Decklin saw the flash of two Appaloosas, heard a familiar voice: "We should break up into smaller groups and continue . . ."

"Lieutenant Holly, I was just telling the sergeant here," interrupted Hib, "that I think our man has made good his escape."

"Whaa—tt . . . ? started the dull-witted Given Holly, pulling rein on his spotted gelding. "You said . . ."

"I don't care what I told you. I want you to take the men back to camp. Miss Booth and I'll follow later . . ."

"But sir," broke in Corporal Gills Holly, kneeing his Appaloosa closer, "he might make contact with Sheridan!"

"I gave an order, Lieutenant—see that it's carried out! And control your brother's tongue!"

"If I may say so, Colonel," began Given Holly, "it might be wise to let a few men scout these hills. I know of at least two trappers' cabins he could hole up in . . ."

"Given's right," chimed in Gills. "If you want, we'll stay . . ."

"You're taking this command back to camp, Lieutenant Holly! And that's that!"

"But sir, he's on foot and shot. He can't be far . . ."

"One more remark out of you, Lieutenant Holly, and I'll slap an insubordinate rap on you! I gave an *order*. *You* carry it out!" Hib forced the words through clenched teeth. The twins had their hands

crossed over their saddle fronts, just staring at him.
"We—ll? What are you waiting for? *A train?*"

For a moment the sun-filled woods were quiet except for the noises of the winded horses and chirping
birds. The Holly twins glared hard at their colonel
and Lieutenant Given Holly gritted a low, "We'll go.
But I say you're wrong." He spun his horse, ordered
the troop forward and nodded his brother closer to
him. After they exchanged a few words, they both
read their C.O. with another long glance, and a cold,
slit-eyed grin. Then they struck heels to their Appaloosas and caught up to the troop. After a short space,
they let the troop lope on as they pulled rein in the
shadowy trees and sat motionless, watching the
unsuspecting Lieutenant Walker Decklin edge from
his hiding place. The twins weren't close enough to
hear what was being said, but they saw all that was
necessary.

Decklin smiled, leaning hard against the cedar.
"You can be a truthful liar, Hib, when you have to.
Now tell me what you've done with Aldis . . ."

Hib laughed. "She's a sly one . . . just like Susan.
I sent the Holly twins out to pick her up. But the
little fool took to the hills like a scared rabbit. Guess
she's lost 'round here someplace."

"If you've hurt her . . ."

Julie interrupted. "Just what do *you* intend doing
with *us?*"

Decklin ignored her and said to Hib, "Unbuckle
your gun belt, and hang it across your saddle . . .
and back away from it."

Hib fumbled with his belt. "You'll never make it with that map." He grinned. "The Holly twins ain't as dumb as they look. You're dead on your feet and won't lie down. Those twins will wait around until you drop out of the saddle. Be sensible . . . make a deal with me."

"I've had a bellyful of *your* deals!" He moved toward the chestnut, leaned hard against it, all the while facing Hib and Julie. Slowly putting his leveled rifle under his hanging right arm, he reached up with his left hand for Hib's Navy Colt. Making sure it was loaded, he tossed his rifle to Hib, who instantly snatched at it.

"Here," Decklin said, "see of you can fix the trigger. The horse busted it when he stepped on it."

Hib was mad enough to chew dirt as he scowled down at the smashed trigger guard. It was all will power that pulled Decklin in the saddle.

"Stop him, Hib," urged Julie.

"You'll never make it. You'll be cut off before you reach Sheridan!"

"Maybe I don't want to *see* Sheridan . . ."

"Now you're talking, Walk! There's enough gold for all three of us . . . split it with us . . . come on, Walk, be a sport! Remember the good ole days we've had together . . . It could be like that again . . ."

Lieutenant Decklin smiled. "But over my dead body . . . that's the way *you'd* plan it, wouldn't you?"

"Ah, come on, Walk. You know me better'n that."

"I don't know you any more, Hib," Lieutenant

Decklin said with slow dignity. "I doubt very much if I ever knew you."

"Ah, come on, Walk, I don't owe the Confederacy nothing. For sure, *you* don't owe the Union a thing!"

At hearing those words, Julie had taken a backward step from Hib. Her eyes became saucer wide. Her hand crept up to her throat. *"Hib,"* she cried, "all these months I thought *you* wanted that map for the Cause . . ."

Hib laughed again. "You're right, Julie. I wanted it for the cause . . . *my cause.*" His laughter died. "My dear," he added, "if you don't know Colonel Viking by now, you better start walking away from me." His eyes looked like two rocks in an icy stream. "Stick with me and I'll give you all the things you could ever want."

He took his eyes off the woman and looked up at the lieutenant. "Well, Walk, all you have to do is turn your back and walk away from the Union—just like your name . . . walk away. You *don't* owe the Union a thing!"

Jamming the revolver in his belt, Decklin reached down over the chestnut's shoulder for the gray's reins; his voice was steady. "I owe my conscience something."

"You fool!"

Julie's shrill voice cried out again, *"Hib!* I can't believe you'd be a traitor to the Southern Cause! You know how bad we need that gold . . . With it we can . . ."

"I hate to disillusion you," broke in Decklin.

"But don't start spending it. Remember I have the map. Why fight over a bone you'll never get?" He touched heels to the chestnut.

"Don't be too sure," growled Hib after him. "I'm not dead yet!"

"Neither am I," Decklin called back over his shoulder.

Farther down the trail, the Holly twins backed into the trees and let Lieutenant Walker Decklin get a head start. Then they circled Hib and Julie and took up the lieutenant's trail themselves.

Riding across the heat-hazed, cottonwood-studded flats, Walker Decklin rode like an outlaw . . . every now and then looking over his shoulder. And every time he did, a shiver of uneasiness, of vague foreboding, ran its course through him.

Pressing into the thickety south, he knew he had to travel hard to outwit Hib; but he needed to stretch out somewhere . . . get some rest. He pulled rein in a dense pine thicket, and let the horses blow; then, taking the soiled envelope from his tunic pocket, he studied it as if it were a two-headed calf.

His mind settled upon the contents beyond the thin covering of the envelope, and he felt a thrill of satisfaction.

All it would take would be a quick tear; the gold map would be his . . . his, Aldis's and Joel's. They could . . . oh the things they could do.

Rustling noise, farther back in the thickets, broke his train of thoughts. He sat motionless, wondering if he had actually heard the fragment of sound or if his mind was playing tricks on him. Quickly he replaced the envelope, and his hand went to the gun in his belt.

He glanced about, eyes shifting right and left, but not moving his head. Here and there he saw a clearing, like an island of light, among the dark waves of continuous treetops.

If there had been a sound, some audible movement to break him out of his thoughts this abrupt way, he could not hear it now. He waited, listening, distrusting even the rustling whisper of the wind that began bending the tall grasses.

The gray horse he was leading was becoming restive, straining at its reins, spooking at make-believe shadows.

He knew scouting Confederates could well be in the vicinity and gave thought to turning the skittish gray loose. But if he did, it would signal his whereabouts; he tugged on the gray's lead reins and found it awkward to hold the gun at the same time.

Unexpectedly the gray nickered and sucked back. Decklin was pulled off-balance as he stretched from the saddle to hold onto the reins. Then the reins were violently torn out of his hand, and he heard the slamming report of a rifle; instantaneously the gray took off at a fast run.

Kicking heels to the chestnut, he threw a snap shot towards his rear trail and leaped his horse deeper into the thickets. Bending low over the gelding's shoulder, he looked back and caught a glimpse of two Appaloosas.

The Holly twins, crashing through the thickets after him, sent two more shots in his direction; both shots missed.

Then he lost sight of the Confederates as he galloped out of the brush into a creek bed, the shallow waters only coming up to the chestnut's knees.

He rode the length of the creek for half a mile before he splashed out; looking over his shoulder, he was satisfied he had lost the twins. A sigh of exhaustion came from him. His shoulders sagged. He knew he had to find rest somewhere, and reined the chestnut up the rocky trail.

Bright morning sunshine dried the rain-drenched grass. The warm-washed sky was filled with billowy white masses of wind-spun clouds, tinged with a reddish transparency that enveloped the earth.

A hot wind began in the north and blew steady southward as the day progressed. The pain in his shoulder took on a steady throbbing; his mouth felt raw and dry. Grass underfoot became glass brittle. The air took on a strange, strong, steady blow; a low roar rose from the forests. The clouds spread over the valley he rode into, rolling swiftly and low. Then the wind swelled to a mourning, moaning windy wail.

Without realizing it, Lieutenant Walker Decklin kept his chestnut pointed always toward the south . . . toward Joplin.

Finally the last bit of blue sky yielded to the onsweep of the clouds. Like angry surf, the pale gleams of gray swept beyond the southern rampart of the valley. The gale swept down with a hollow, unearthly howl, shrilling as it came. It had no counterpart of the sounds of elements. It was not of earth or of life; it was more like a grief and agony that spilled over the valley.

For the first time, his glance went into the distance. He saw, out across the vast, tree-mantled sweep of solidly timbered hills surrounding him, the thing that made him abruptly stop his horse. The warm wind swiftly whistled all around. At first, he didn't believe what he saw . . . but there it was, a stark reality. The sun-lit sky now became the color of blood and death, the heavens lighting up like a bonfire.

Lieutenant Walker Decklin was watching the south lands being set ablaze!

Miles farther north, and on a higher rim, a grayish pall of smoke lay over the forests. For a moment it looked as if a giant low-hanging cloud had dropped from the sky. Even as he watched, it fanned out before the wind, growing in density. Then his eye caught another rise of smoke a short distance from the first, and flames were leaping one upon another.

He said to himself, "The fools, they're trying to cut me off—and burning up the whole country! *The fools!*"

Then a strange laugh was born deep within his chest and rose to his lips. He threw his head back and let the touch of unreason have its way. When it was gone, he saw another stand of timber become engulfed in flames and smoke; and another; and another, as if a great unseen hand were tossing matches out of the heavens.

The hot cyclone wind kept picking up the fires and

distributing the flames in great masses, circling him within its realm. He spurred toward the south, and within half an hour his eyes were starting to burn from the creeping haze of smoke.

Crackling noise before him made him pull in the chestnut with a frightened jerk on the reins; instantly he kneed into the tangled wall of an old dark funnel of a deer run.

He was sure that there was movement in the brush not far ahead. . . . Then his ears caught a faint sound!

There could be no mistaking *that* noise; it was a muffled human cough!

The whining of a bullet slapped the cedar beside his head, and he heard the sharp report of a rifle. Immediately he slid from the saddle, grimacing at the pain the quick movement brought him, and dived through a tangle of oak shrubs by the side of the deer run.

He focused his vision through the filtered sun of the forest's darkness and could just make out a huddled shape beyond a cannon-shattered cedar tree; then the form was gone.

He waited and listened. . . . The slap of running feet came to him.

Someone was racing along the ridge in front of him, intent on swift escape, and Decklin felt sure it was either one of the Holly twins or one of Colonel Viking's men.

Decklin cut through the thickets and worked around to head off the man; he saw the shadowy form running toward him, and he stumbled out to block him. The runner wheeled to the side and raised a thick-barreled rifle, trying to swipe it out at Decklin's face.

Decklin threw himself at the narrow-shouldered man; both fell to the earth with breath-dispelling grunts. Decklin pinned the struggling body between his knees and clamped his foot on the rifle that glinted dully on the sunlit path; but his squirming captive kept reaching for it until, with his stiff right arm, Decklin pressed the large-brimmed hat-covered head into the dirt with a hard shove.

Abruptly, the body twisted beneath Decklin and began pounding at his wounded shoulder. Lieutenant Decklin lost his hold on the striking, twisting body, and his captive jumped to the advantage and leaped to his feet.

Decklin reached out for his victim's legs and pulled him back down to the ground. His breath was knocked from him by the weight of the body that fell completely on top of him.

High over the trees, the bright sun filtered through a break in the woods, streaking the land below with light and darkness. A strip of light fell on Decklin's captive as the big hat was wrenched from his head. A cascade of nut-brown hair fell about sloping shoulders.

Lieutenant Walker Decklin gasped in amazement, "Aldis!"

CHAPTER FIFTEEN

"I never thought I'd see you again," she murmured, wriggling from him and coming to her knees. Then she was grabbing him by the arm and tugging. "Hurry, Walk—get up. We have to beat the fire to the creek!"

He let himself be helped to his feet. "Why . . . why did you shoot at me?"

"Thought you were one of those twins after me."

He looked at her taut, fire-smudged face.

"Did they harm you?" He grabbed her by the shoulders. "Tell me!"

"Didn't give 'em a chance," she said, and noticed the scarlet stain on his shoulder. A frown wrinkled between her eyes. "Hib do that?"

Decklin nodded.

"Does it hurt much?"

"Bullet is still in there . . . needs to come out. Do you think you can do it?"

She gasped, then quickly said, "Let's hurry to where I've been staying—it's not far from here. Those twins won't think I'd go back there. We'll have to outrun this fire, though. Hurry." She let him hold onto her arm as she steadied him over to the chestnut.

Sunlight and smoky haze struck full on her. He noticed the man's clothing she had on—blue trousers that clung tightly to her thighs revealed shapely limbs, made his eyes wander slowly down to her knees, then her ankles and the buckskin moccasins on tiny feet. Quickly his eyes roamed up her rounded hips, beyond her thin waist circled by a narrow beaded belt, beyond her breasts beneath the white cotton shirt, and came to rest on her smiling eyes. It was the first time he had seen her in men's clothing, and he liked what he saw.

She let him mount first and reached her hands behind her head to tie the yellow ribbon that had become loose; she looked back at her floppy hat on the ground, shrugged at it, and quickly tucked a toe in the near stirrup Decklin had made ready and swung up behind him.

Exhaustion had completely taken over Lieutenant Decklin by the time they reached the winding creek. Vaguely he remembered splashing it, riding up to a trapper's log cabin that swayed crazily to one side. It had been all Aldis MacKay could manage to get him into the cabin to the bed. He must have gone to sleep, or blacked out, for he never remembered her removing the bullet from his shoulder.

He lay on his stomach now, on the plank cot, his left arm dangling over the edge, his fingers touching the sod floor. Then the smell of rabbit stew came to him and he opened his eyes.

The cabin was dark as a cobweb-filled cave, with

the exception of a small fire glow in one corner. Aldis was hovering over a rusty black kettle suspended above the crackling fire on the stone hearth.

He turned over with a groan, and immediately felt that the paralyzing effect on his right arm was gone. But he was weak.

She turned and smiled at him. "Awake already?"

"Did you shoot that rabbit?"

"I'm not that stupid! One shot would have had the Confederates up here in no time at all . . ." She put her hands on her hips, cocked her head to one side and smiled wider. "My dear Lieutenant . . . don't you know I can set a good snare . . . for man or beast?"

He let her bantering pass and asked, "How long have I been sleeping?"

"Only about an hour or so."

He rubbed his left hand across his bare chest and up to the padded wad tied against his right shoulder. "I give you a bad time?"

"Not very." She turned and busied herself with the soup kettle. "We'll have to eat out of the pot. Mind?"

He didn't answer; he was too busy fumbling for his shirt and jacket and gun, lying on the floor four feet from him. Tossing his legs over the edge of the cot, he got his shirt and began rummaging through it. He stood and swayed on his feet.

Hearing his movement, she turned and quickly protested, "Walk, don't! You'll reopen your wound!"

"Where's the envelope?"

"What envelope? Maybe you lost it. Or maybe it's

still in your jacket pocket. Get back to bed. I'll look for it." She came and put a restraining hand on his arm.

He shoved it from him with a vicious push. "Aldis . . . that envelope is our whole future . . ."

She took a step back. "What's in it?" and picked up his dirty tunic and began poking into pockets.

He looked up at her, his eyes glassy with pain. "A gold map," he said calmly.

Her face tightened. "Walk . . . it couldn't belong to you! Where'd you get it?"

"Major Mitchel asked me to deliver it to Sheridan."

Her fingers touched paper. She pulled out the tan envelope, held it up. "This it?"

He grabbed it, dropping his shirt in his anxiety. "That's it." He started to tear open the flap.

"You can't do that!" she said, reaching for it. "If Major Mitchel trusted you to deliver it to General Sheridan . . . don't you see, Walk, it'll exonerate you of this terrible lie you've gotten yourself into!"

"Mitchel's dead by now. I don't owe anybody or anything—*nothing!* I've gone through Hell for this stinkin' piece of paper." He held the envelope up. "I think I'm entitled to something other than just a clear record!"

"You can't mean that!"

"With every drop of blood in my body, I mean it." His voice was low, but he held his head stiff and high above her.

She stepped back another pace; flickering firelight

danced on her soiled face. "You break that seal, Walk," she said, "and your conscience will put you through a worse Hell." She looked directly into his eyes, and said, "But I'll go along with whatever you decide upon."

She picked up his shirt and came closer. "Put it on," she said, trying to change the subject. "You'll get a chill."

He let her work his arms into it, exchanging the envelope from hand to hand, all the while watching her face. Then he said breathlessly, "You would, wouldn't you?"

Her hands were fumbling with the button at his throat.

"A good wife follows her husband," she murmured.

"To Hell?"

"And back again." Her words came as a whisper.

"Aldis . . ." he muttered with a muffled cry, "I love you . . . all the way."

For an instant she lowered her eyelids, then she tipped her head back and looked up at him. "All the way."

He made a sound deep in his throat and drew her to him. Finally he held her away from him, staring down at her with a strange expression in his face.

"It's a long way back."

"From where?"

"Hell . . ."

She smiled. "Together, we'll find a short cut."

He looked at her. "I think you would," he said, smiling.

After a time, Aldis returned to the fire.

Decklin continued to stand in the middle of the dusty, cobweb-filled shack. He glanced up from the sealed envelope and only noticed now that complete darkness had fallen. He could see the night through the cracks in the logs. Forest smoke lingered all about in a heat-hung haze.

He said to her, "This isn't your home?"

"Of course not. When Pa got killed at Willow Gap, I began living with the Ladies' Welfare Association and let Pa's farm go to ruin . . . but I like to go out there and linger with my memories. That's when those Holly twins . . ."

He nodded and went to the door opening, where the plank door hung akimbo off its leather hinges. The sky was a blood red. Crowning trees to the south could still be heard popping in the fire. The barren lands below spread under the scarlet moon like an immense sheet of unbleached linen. And he said to her, without bothering to turn around and face her, "Aldis . . . I don't know what to do," and looked down at the unopened envelope gripped in his fist.

"My conscience tells me to do one thing. . . . I want to do the opposite." His glance swept across her face, searching for some sign. He said quietly, "Aldis . . . who will you bet on? The man or the man's conscience?" and looked directly into her eyes.

Her eyes were as clear and cool as mountain water

when the sunlight is upon it and golden flecks come
and go in its brown depths. Without hesitation, she
replied, "The man's conscience."

Slowly he shook his head, staring at her almost
blankly for a moment.

"You lost the bet . . ."

"No, I didn't," she murmured, coming over to
him.

She stood there with her hand on his arm; then
her eyes glanced over his shoulder and they flashed
wide in fright. She screamed.

Shuffling boots behind Decklin spun him around;
the Holly twins were hunched in the doorway, their
guns leveled at him.

"You gave us a wild chase, Yank," said Given
Holly, stepping in and poking his .44 in the lieutenant's stomach. "But it's all over now." He laughed—
a shallow, weak sound. "Give me that letter."

CHAPTER SIXTEEN

Aldis knew that Decklin's gun on the floor was too far away to try for, and the thought of them killing Decklin threw panic in her.

She glanced down at a smoldering log, sticking out from under the boiling kettle. She moved from Decklin and bent for it as the twins lumbered inside the shack.

Given's shallow eyes fastened on the envelope in Lieutenant Decklin's hand, and the tip of the Confederate's tongue flicked out and touched his dry lips. "Yank," he said, "you want to give it to me, or do I shoot your hand off and take it?"

"You would, wouldn't you?"

"He would," chimed in Gills. "But in case he wouldn't . . . you darn well know I will." He shifted his gaze over at the girl and saw what she was doing. He shuffled toward her. Decklin took a quick step toward him.

"Don't," warned Given, pressing the gun against Decklin's stomach and stepping aside to let his twin get at the girl. He tried not to take his eyes off Decklin, but had to when Gills' alarm sounded. "Watch it! She's goin' to throw a burnin' log!"

Given took his eyes off Decklin and saw the girl's hand and blazing log half raised above her head. He

163

yelled at Gills, "Shoot her!" but Decklin had seen his chance and took it.

His fist lashed out, raking Given along the jaw as he leaped forward with the speed of a cat. He dropped the envelope as his left fist rammed into the Confederate's stomach, driving all the wind out of the man's lungs in a gasping belch, and doubling him over.

Then Decklin rose on his toes, bringing up his fist as an open-handed stiff board and clubbed it down against the back of the Confederate's neck. Given Holly crashed face down on the floor at his feet, and lay still.

Aldis side-stepped Gills and threw the burning log at him. It caught him smack across the chest; he screamed as if an explosion had taken place on his person, and screamed all the louder when he watched his gray jacket begin to smoke. He dropped his gun and snatched off his coat, but his skin was already singed. His screams lengthened and loudened, like the repeated cry of a cage-trapped buzzard.

The cabin was in shadowy darkness, the only light coming from the hearth. Being closest to the envelope, Decklin scooped it up and was going for the gun when a voice from the door stopped him.

"Leave it lay, Walk."

Lieutenant Decklin reeled about and saw Hib and Julie framed in the doorway, the runaway gray horse standing behind them, its sides heaving from the grueling ride it had just made.

Decklin straightened and said grimly, "You never

give up . . . do you, Hib?" and looked down at one of the twins' rifles Hib had snatched from a horse outside, its leveled bore never wavering.

"Not when I want something bad enough." Hib grinned. "Like that envelope you're holding."

Gills Holly was still slapping at the fire on his shirt. But when he saw who the intruder was, he dived for his fallen gun, cursing. "Colonel Viking . . . my brother and I tracked the Yank! That map he's got is ours!"

"Corporal Holly," snapped Hib, "the only thing you got is this!" His rifle roared in one ear-splitting blast. The Confederate broke in two, then fell his full length on the sod floor, a crimson stain spreading an inch above his belt buckle.

Hib turned to Decklin. "That shows I'm not foolin', Walk. Now do you hand that envelope over?"

Lieutenant Decklin's eyes narrowed in the flickering light. "No," he replied mildly, as would a mother telling her child he couldn't have any more candy because it will make him sick.

Julie pushed past Hib. "Walk, you better do like he says."

Lieutenant Walker Decklin slowly moved his head from side to side, all the while looking Hib in the eyes. "No."

Hib moistened his lips with his tongue, and met Decklin's eyes with his own gimlet glance, sharp as the point of a screw. When he started toward Decklin, the lieutenant stood his ground, but put both hands behind his back, cupping the envelope there, daring Hib to take it. He spread his legs apart to keep his balance, preparing for Hib's attack he felt was sure to come.

Hib reached out and grabbed Lieutenant Walker Decklin by the shirt front with one hand and pushed the rifle barrel up against his temple with the other. He roared with a bull-like loudness and fury as he pulled the lieutenant closer to him. "I could kill you!"

Lieutenant Decklin clenched harder on the envelope behind his back and stiffened his shoulders against the strain of the man's fist on his chest. "You did, back at Camp Stillwater."

A breathless silence followed as the two men stared into each other's eyes; each determined to have his way.

It took a woman to break that terrible muteness, in a manner in which only a woman can. Aldis MacKay screamed at Hib, "You're insane!" She swung back toward the kettle, reaching for the metal ladle she'd been stirring the boiling broth with. Jerking it out with a full scoop of scalding soup, she flung it at the Confederate's face.

Hib yelped in pain and fright and let his hold on Decklin loosen, as he dropped his rifle and clawed at his eyes. Decklin pushed away, wiping at the hot liquid that had splashed on his chest.

Given Holly was trying to get to his feet, crouching on all fours, head hanging between his extended arms.

"Let's get outa here!" yelled Decklin, grabbing for Aldis.

Julie, puzzled at the sudden outburst of action, was standing in the door arch. Aldis made one swipe at the woman and pulled off Julie's cloak, yelling at her, "You're just like Hib . . . no good!" and doubled up her fist and let it fly into Julie's parted mouth.

Julie fell back, and an all-woman hatred screamed its vengeance in her voice: "You back-hills garbage picker!" She took another jab to the face, this time an open-handed smack that threw her to the floor, with Aldis jumping on her and shredding her gown and flesh with fingers that curved and stiffened and twisted like the talons of a hawk; but Julie's own nails were jerking the thin shirt from Aldis's back.

Before Decklin had gathered his wits to stop the women, Julie had wrenched free from Aldis and was rising to one knee and raking with her ten arched fingers. The swift movement ripped Aldis's shirt front down to the circle of her belt.

For second the two women stood panting on the scuffed-up sod floor. Then Aldis tried to leap at Julie again, only to have Decklin wrap his arms about her and drag her from the cabin.

Julie was screaming and running to Hib on the floor. "Get up . . . get up! They're getting away!"

Grabbing the closest horse, one of the twins' Appaloosas, Decklin swung into the saddle, said, "We'll ride double on this one. The others look too far winded." Quickly, he pulled Aldis up behind.

"Look," said Aldis, pointing to the south, "the fires are still raging . . . You can't get through to Sheridan . . ."

"I told you . . . I'm not going to find Sheridan."

He felt her stiffen, and he slammed heels to the horse.

"I thought," she said, clinging to his waist, "when you wouldn't give Hib the envelope, you were going to try and clear your record . . . Where are we going, if not to Sheridan?"

For a few long-strided lopes he didn't answer; when he did his voice was flat and in it was a faint grumble: "I thought you didn't care where you lived . . . Heaven or Hell!"

She didn't reply, but he felt her hands moving across his waist at his back as if she was removing something from her body. Then he felt the twisting movement of her right arm and felt the horse gather up a sudden burst of speed. Glancing over his shoulder, he saw she was smiling and quirting the Appaloosa with her belt.

That was her answer.

CHAPTER SEVENTEEN

They were less than fifteen minutes on the trail when the fire-tinted moon rode in the blood-streaked sky like a shadow lamp, flooding the land with the sad, soft light of wasted dreams.

Lieutenant Walker Decklin made out the dark confines of a ragged canyon, along the northwest rim of which they galloped.

Aldis turned her head over her shoulder; she sucked in her breath with a deep gasp. "Walk," she panted, "we're being followed already!"

The lieutenant hipped slightly in the saddle and made out two riders, riding double. "Hib and Julie . . ."

And she heard him moan; then he gave a shallow laugh and pointed a tired hand toward another racing horse; and Aldis made out the beefy form of Given Holly about a half mile behind them, skirting Hib and Julie and drawing closer to themselves.

Then came the nerve-shattering volley of distant cannons booming toward the north . . .

Then the south . . .

Lieutenant Decklin urged the Appaloosa down into the canyon, hoping to shake their pursuers. The broken plateau sloped down to a rent in the earth.

Fire-singed cedar and pine burned their nostrils; brush grew thin in the rocky ground; long slants of gray stone tilted down the canyon ridge. The bottom of the deep gorge could not be seen, but across it the opposite wall loomed up, ragged and split, green and gray, where the fires hadn't touched.

They reached the bottom with a four-legged, stiff jump of the Appaloosa, throwing Decklin's body back against the girl, who cried out her surprise at reaching the base of their descent so soon.

"Don't worry," Decklin mumbled to her. "There won't be any other fools to chance the ride down that hill tonight."

It was a long gamble, this dash down the canyon floor. One wrong slip of the horse's hoofs and they would be sent sprawling—at the mercy of their followers on the rim.

At last, Lieutenant Decklin was forced to slow down to a trot, then a walk, bordering the washed-out cracks and rocks on the slippery stone floor.

High above on the canyon ridge, Given Holly pulled up his Appaloosa and watched the two below. The moon was throwing off sufficient light for him to draw his rifle to his shoulder. The Confederate took careful aim and pulled the trigger. The shot cut the night like a saber, screaming its echoing way down into the canyon and bouncing back.

Decklin's horse shied with a squeal of fright as the bullet chipped a rock to the front of it and ricocheted off, sending splinters of stone against the Appaloosa's chest and off fore-shoulder. Without an upward glance, Decklin kicked heels to the horse, unmindful of the cracks and gullies opening up about the horse's feet, and headed for the archway of the canyon half a mile away.

He could hear the pounding of Given's horse above, racing to cut him off.

The rippling muscles of the Appaloosa gelding told Decklin of the strain he carried as the animal rimmed this crack and that. Then out of the darkness flashed a ragged, yawning crevice and the Appaloosa quickly shied at it, only to brush against an unseen rock. The gelding stumbled as its outreaching near forefoot struck it. With a jerk, Decklin pulled hard on the reins; Aldis held tighter to his belt. The Appaloosa gained his footing, only to step into the crevice he had shied from and plunged to the ground with an earth-slamming grunt. The plunge sent Lieutenant Decklin and the girl sprawling over the gelding's head.

Lieutenant Decklin was rising to his knees when, suddenly, Given Holly was riding down on him and Aldis, and haunch-sliding his Appaloosa to a stop, a cloud of smoky dust swirling about him.

The Confederate grinned. "Hard fall you took, Yank," he said, dismounting and walking over to Decklin, all the while keeping his .44 pointed at the middle button on Decklin's shirt.

Decklin made a move to get up, but Given Holly pushed him back with a boot as he reached down and took the envelope that was sticking out from the lieutenant's belt.

The Confederate's sharp-glancing grin gave the impression of extreme efficiency; his voice, with its hint of sardonic amusement, was like a trumpet call to battle.

"Like a horse with a broken leg, Yank," said Given Holly, "I could put you out of your misery. But what's the use. Sometimes I think livin's harder for some." He laughed his shrill laugh, holstered his .44 and turned to mount.

He was much too interested in obtaining the gold map; he didn't hear the horse come up behind him until a voice called out, "Lieutenant Holly, you leave a trail like an elephant in three feet of snow. Now drop your gun and hand over that envelope!"

The three of them turned, their gazes pinpointing Hib, Julie clinging to him on the back of their mount.

Then Lieutenant Given Holly was wheeling to the left, snatching for the gun at his side, at the same time yammering, "Colonel Viking! Damn you . . . you killed my brother!"

Hib fired the instant Given spun, catching the tall Confederate in the chest. Hib hit the ground just as Given's knees buckled; and he watched his lieutenant pitch forward on his face, sending a useless slug into the soil.

Julie slid down from the horse and hurried over to the fallen Confederate, going through his pockets as if she were at a rummage sale.

"Just what do you think you're doing?" Hib

snapped, rushing over and knocking her roughly aside. Seeing she had the envelope clutched in her fist, he grabbed it. "Here," he growled, "give that to me! It's mine!"

"*No!*" she insisted. "It belongs to the Confederacy!"

Hib's eyes narrowed. "Julie," he gritted, "you're the first woman who ever slapped my face." He rubbed his fingers across his remembering hurt of embarrassment. "You're on your own from here on out. Now get away from me!"

He swung his gaze over on Decklin and Aldis. That small smile of his turned up his dry lips and his rifle leveled.

Lieutenant Decklin began to scramble to his feet, but the fall had sapped his energy, and re-opened his shoulder wound. He crumpled back as Hib said, "Stay there, Walk," his voice queerly soft. "No sense to press your luck." He moved toward the crouching lieutenant, his laborious walk like the creeping of a beetle, the legs alone moving with horrid industry while the body glided evenly.

The ragged Unionist took hold of the woman's hand as she knelt beside him in the rocky dust. "Hib," he said, "give me the envelope."

Hib Kinsman moved away from that beckoning hand, and slowly shook his head. "Nope," was his reply. It was only when he looked in Lieutenant Decklin's eyes that he realized the man was someone out of the ordinary. And in that instant, he knew if he was ever to find peace from those eyes, he would have to kill the man behind them.

He began dropping the barrel of the rifle, to make one precise bullet count. Swift and painless; he owed that much to the lieutenant.

Lieutenant Decklin lowered his hand, passing the back of it across his forehead as if to dispel a cloud from his mind. "Hib," he said softly, watching the bore of the rifle center his head, "you're too late with your bullet. Like I said before, you killed me back at Stillwater. What worries you now isn't *me* . . . isn't knowing that if you don't bury me, I'll track you down. What worries you is *your* conscience . . . and *you* say you have none." He rocked his head to and fro. "Pull the trigger and see how long it'll take before you put a bullet in your own brain. And Hib, when you kill yourself, *you* won't be the one pulling the trigger . . . it'll be *your* conscience, and that'll be me."

Lieutenant Walker Decklin kept looking up at Hib, staring at him with unblinking eyes. The stunted smile on Hib's lips froze; his face became completely colorless and his lips turned the tint of gray mold. Those lips hardly moved when he said, "I'm sorry it has to be this way, Walk . . ."

Aldis began sobbing and clutching the lieutenant's arm; Decklin began pushing her from him. Hib Kinsman's drawling voice pushed back the woman's sobs. "Just for the record, Walk," he said, "weren't you *really* going to keep the map for yourself?"

"Yes . . . and no . . ."

Hib's lips broke into a smile, and the smile into a hoarse laugh. "Oh, I get it. *Your* conscience again . . . good ole *Fort Hell.*"

"You might say that," returned Decklin, and thought he heard the thunder of horses' hoofs coming from the south. He cocked his head to the side.

Hib's forehead wrinkled; he had heard the sound, too.

The noise rumbled like a full cavalry.

Julie had gotten to her feet and stood spread-legged behind Hib. She called to him, "You can't mean what you just said," she whimpered. "You promised to marry me, Hib . . . you got to! *You* got to!"

Hib snapped her a glance over his shoulder and whipped, "I don't *got* to do nothin'!"

"Except shoot me," taunted Decklin.

Hib shoved the envelope in his belt and kept staring down at Decklin. He felt the cold sweat beginning to bead on his face . . . run down his neck . . . down his chest. The more he stared at the lieutenant, kneeling on the ground too weak to rise to his feet, the more the sight of the man sent tiny prickling movements up and down his spine. A breath of warm air from the smoky atmosphere sent a shiver through him as if an icy hand had touched him. Then he was bringing up his rifle and holding it across his chest like a shield, his slim fingers twisting and locking themselves nervously about the stock and barrel. When he brought his eyes up again, he saw that the lieutenant's hadn't shifted, and he doubted if those frozen sapphires had even blinked. Hib held his gaze on those eyes for an answer as one holds metal in a vise for testing.

Finally, he brought his rifle up to his shoulder and took careful aim at the lieutenant's head again.

Lieutenant Decklin's eyes neither slitted nor widened; they just keep staring up at the Confederate. And his voice had a strange effect of quietness:

"I see, Hib . . . You're in *Fort Hell* now."

That was all it took—eight words, spaced right, and in the proper tone.

Hib Kinsman muttered a low, "Ah, Hell," thrust the rifle down to the ground with a vicious slam, and then kicked it away from him. Then he wheeled to mount his horse.

"Don't leave me, Hib," Julie whimpered. "Don't leave me!"

She reached down for the rifle Hib had thrown aside. Her voice had even lost its begging whine. "Hib, take me with you." And then she blushed. She said, a little breathlessly, "I'm going to have your baby."

He turned slightly, his features going blank. "I told you where to go. Now get gone." He shifted back to the saddle and fumbled with the stirrup.

Before Lieutenant Decklin could shout a warning, Julie had leveled the rifle and screamed at Hib,

"You're coming with me!" She pulled the trigger just as the Confederate colonel spun around, taking the bullet in the stomach.

For the space of a minute, the Confederate kept his upright posture, but he stood like a stalled ox, spreading wide his legs to keep his balance. His hands kept clutching at the crimson spreading above his belt buckle and staining the envelope tucked there.

Then Colonel Hib Viking took a step toward the woman holding the smoking rifle. His lips parted to say something, but no sound came. His shoulders sagged and he folded at the waist, slowly going down to his knees.

When he lay fully stretched out on the ground, he looked like a man who had been searching for a place to rest and had found it.

Before Hib crumpled to the earth, Lieutenant Decklin had scrambled to his feet and was stumbling over to him, but not before Julie had reached the downed man and retrieved the envelope.

Julie backed away from them, eyes wide, her mouth a tight line crossing her twitching face. "I warned him," she whimpered. "I warned him." She started to level the rifle at Decklin and Aldis.

The sound of cavalry crashing the underbrush of the canyon came to them more clearly now, and within seconds the horsemen's galloping approach surrounded them as one hundred and twenty-nine Unionists, attracted by the gunshots, rode up to where they clustered about a Union lieutenant kneeling beside a Confederate Colonel.

Seeing the cavalry was Union, Julie quickly hid the envelope behind her and threw the rifle into the shadows, her blue eyes flashing defiance.

CHAPTER EIGHTEEN

Lieutenant Walker Decklin eased Hib's shoulders to the ground and managed to come to a wobbly stand. He looked briefly at the Unionist reining a massive big-boned black closer to him; then his gaze went back to the man twisting in pain at his feet. Memories of Hib, ever since he could cherish memories, flashed before him . . .

. . . eating crackers in the same bed with him . . .

. . . sharing orchard-stolen apples with him and Joel . . .

. . . Hib giving him his first pair of spurs . . .

. . . helping him to his feet, when his first green bronc bucked him off . . .

. . . wrapping up his ribs when a loco steer gored him . . .

. . . walking twenty-odd miles in the snow, for a doctor, when fever from a snakebite threatened to take his life . . .

. . . going to church dances together . . .

. . . the picnic get-togethers . . .

. . . Hib introducing Susan and Aldis to him . . . and Julie . . .

. . . rifle practice behind the barn!

That seemed to have been when the good times ended—back behind the barn, when Joel got crippled.

The happy experiences of knowing a man are always fresh to look back upon . . . not the sad times . . . the bad times. And memory when it broods over the pleasant joys of knowing a man is like the air of spring, opening new flowers. All the mean memories should be plowed into the soil to act as organic matter, to enrich a man's character. But the remembrance of hellish days cannot be forever excluded; they come to a man's mind like shadows; they push back all the good recollections and they stand, like black velvet mountains of mournfulness.

That was Lieutenant Walker Decklin's feeling now, as he sighed and looked down at Hib . . .

"We heard shooting," said the man on the big black, and the sound of the Unionist's voice boomed like a cannon in Decklin's ears; he had to shake his head to bring himself back to the present. The voice came again: "What's the trouble?"

It was too dark for Lieutenant Decklin to make out the man's face and rank; at least, he wanted to think it was the darkness and not the misty film sheeting his eyes. He heard the cavalry behind this persistent officer on the black horse, their sabers clapping as they checked their mounts in tight rein.

"She took . . . military papers off me . . . shot me . . ." came Hib's shallow whisper at Decklin's feet as the man tried to make a gesture with his hand toward the whimpering Julie.

Whatever feelings Walker Decklin had been experiencing now turned to complete repulsiveness. Hib's words made him ashamed he had ever known him. Decklin was no longer mournful, only embarrassed and ashamed. Even in death, this man would lie for wealth; when now, Hib had it in his power to clear Decklin's record, the man called Hib Kinsman and Colonel Viking would die lacking the pleasure of knowing how it felt to have a conscience. . . .

"He lies!" whipped Julie, backing away from the circle of solemn watchers.

Aldis stepped to Decklin's side, saying, "She's the liar! She has an envelope that belongs to General Sheridan! This man was delivering it!"

The stocky Unionist on that big black kneed the horse closer and said, "I'm Sheridan," with a little chuckle to his voice.

Decklin looked up at the man, noticed his smile was rather melancholy, and watched the general's great drooping mustaches twitch as the man settled deeper in his saddle and gave a tiny cough to clear his throat. Decklin stiffened, and he didn't know how or why he was doing it, but he was saluting.

"Give me the envelope, girl," came Sheridan's calm voice, motioning with his head that he knew she held it behind her. Shade from the man's wide-brimmed campaign hat threw darker shadows about his silvered hair and deep-set eyes. He cleared his throat again. "Tell me, just who was delivering it."

Hib's voice came breathlessly up to the general: "That envelope belongs . . . to . . . me . . ."

"It's mine!" insisted Julie. "You can't take it off me! I won't let you!"

"You lying tramp!" Aldis screamed, rushing forward at Julie.

Decklin grabbed her and held her hands.

"No need to get excited, ladies," grumbled Sheridan, looking at Julie. He reached out a gloved hand and said, "Woman, just give me the article in question and the matter will soon be settled."

Julie Booth treaded forward in a grudging fashion, and handed the general the envelope.

"Now tell me . . . one at a time," came Sheridan's rumbling voice as he looked down at the mud- and blood-stained packet, "just who was the original bearer of this message?"

The canyon echoed with four loud voices speaking at once. The general shook his head. "I only have one pair of ears!" He took a slow breath. There was not much patience left in him. "You, Lieutenant," he nodded at Decklin, a frown wrinkling his forehead as he let his gaze run up and down the lieutenent's ragged uniform, "you resemble a Unionist . . . you tell me!" Sheridan slanted his craggy head to one side and measured the lieutenant with critical eyes.

Walker Decklin took a step forward, swaying as he moved. He clamped his hand over the bloody blotch on his shoulder and tried to straighten. His mouth became an unbending thin line. "Major Mitchel gave me the envelope. The major and I were both prisoners of his." He looked down at Hib and lowered the lashes over his eyes.

Hib saw that Decklin was reluctant to reveal his true identity. He twitched the pain from his face and smiled that cold smile of his and said, "Go ahead, Walk . . . tell the General who I really am." He moved his gaze up to Sheridan and his smile twisted. "I'm *Colonel Viking.*" He laughed, a strange, strained sound.

The general maintained his composure admirably. He focused his interest on Decklin. "Did you shoot this man . . . this Colonel Viking?"

Decklin glanced down at Hib, who was trying to sit up, his voice coming to the lieutenant in a croaking whine: "Walk, work it right . . ." and the whine dropped to a shallow whisper. "Walk . . . there's enough gold for both of us. Say that letter is my personal property . . . or if you don't trust me, say it's yours . . . but, Walk, don't give it up . . . don't be a *fool!*"

Decklin was shaking his head from side to side, watching the man creeping towards him, begging with his voice, his hands, his eyes.

"I'm not going to die, Walk . . ." Hib groaned. "There's too much ahead for me. . . . Don't give up that letter . . . please."

Decklin watched Hib dragging his legs behind him like some giant gray insect.

"No, General Sheridan," came his brisk voice as he stepped back from Hib's reaching hands, "I didn't shoot this man. If I had, he wouldn't be able to be lying now." The fingers that had made their clawing way up the lieutenant's legs lost their hold on Deck-

lin's trousers. Walker Decklin watched Hib slump
down to the dust and lay there, face down in it, sobs
of anger trembling his sagged shoulders.

Decklin glanced down at Hib. "You had your
chance, a long time past," he murmured out of the
depths of a great sadness. "I told you . . . years ago
. . . you were ridin' a horse high, wide and handsome. Someday you'd get bucked off, and there'd be
nobody 'round to pick you up. That time is now,
Hib. I'm sorry."

General Sheridan's voice came to him, but he
hardly heard it. "Lieutenant," said the general,
"what is your name, and your post? Just where did
you come from?"

"Lieutenant Walker Decklin."

The general looked as if he had been slapped
across the face. "You stand there and admit you're
this *Walker Decklin?*"

"I do, sir," Decklin said quite politely and respect-
fully.

Resentment and annoyance sheeted the general's
features. It was even in the pitch of his voice. "Then
you're under arrest!"

CHAPTER NINETEEN

Walker Decklin stood there, looking up at the general. The circle of Unionists surrounded him, bayoneted rifles tipped at his chest.

General Sheridan said, "When my command took over Camp Stillwater, I was given the outline of Colonel Moore's murder. I also have a Lieutenant Walker Decklin's confession to that murder in my possession." He hipped in the saddle and said to his men, "Shoot this man if he tries to escape!"

Walker Decklin's shoulders never slumped. "Sir," he began, feeling Aldis's tight grip on his arm, "the contents of the envelope might explain my innocence."

"I hardly think so!" Sheridan neck-reined his black to the side, a big red-faced man who ruled according to the rigid edicts of the book, if possible, a little more so than Major Mitchel.

Decklin drew in a slow breath, turned his head and looked down at Hib, who had twisted over on his back. He was beginning to feel the rise of his own anger, anger of the lie that had gotten him in this mess. He didn't know that Sheridan had broken the seal on the envelope and was reading one of the letters to himself. Then his face became rigid and he opened the second letter. His face was wine-red with anxiety as his eyes scanned the paper; his lips parted to speak, but no sound came. As he straightened his shoulders, he measured Decklin with critical eyes and said, "You were delivering these papers to me?"

There grew a rebel look about Walker Decklin. For a moment, he studied the question, looking down at Hib, who kept shaking his head and muttering, "Say no . . . say no . . ."

Finally Decklin took his gaze off Hib, rose it to the general and softly said, "Yes, sir."

"He wasn't!" cried Julie, her hand reaching up to the general's knee. "He's lying! That letter is *mine!*"

"Walk," came Hib's faint whisper, "you're not a man . . . you're a damn conscience . . ."

General Sheridan's face was solemn when he handed Julie the two letters and said, "Read them, my dear. Read them out loud."

That outburst of the general's surprised everyone. And it was a weird, strained, unbelieving woman's voice that filled the canyon:

" 'To whom it may concern,' " Julie started the first letter. " 'If the bearer of this packet is captured, it will do the Southern cause no good. For this bearer was an unsuspecting decoy delivering blank papers.' " She said the words twice, not quite believing what she was reading. " 'Blank papers which enabled the true message to get through to the rightful hands of the Unionists. This letter will condone the bearer of all knowledge of not knowing what he was carrying

and why he was carrying it. And what I intended this
bearer to believe he was carrying was purely inten-
tional, so he could distract the enemy from the original messenger. I highly commend Lieutenant Walker
Decklin's courage and bravery. Signed Major
O. M. Mitchel . . . March 22, 1865.' "

Unmindful of the pointed bayonets, Decklin
pushed forward and grabbed the papers from Julie.
The troopers closed him in a tighter circle, cutting
Aldis off from him. Looking at the letter, his whole
body seemed to shrink. Lines etched themselves
deeply into a face turned the color of parchment.

Sheridan looked down at Julie. "My dear," he said,
"there was no meat on the bone you were fighting
over . . . shot a man for . . ." He turned to Decklin. "You see, Lieutenant, I received the true report,
with the gold map and instructions about firing the
countryside around Joplin, this morning. We've already taken back the city . . . the Confederacy is
starting to move out of Richmond. President Davis
has retired from the capitol. One more raid on Richmond, and this hellish war will be ended. We—ll, at
least the commands will cease; we can't be too sure
about the guerrillas. I say sometime next month—
sometime in April—the shooting will be ordered to
a halt."

Decklin wasn't listening; he was looking down at
the blank paper in his hand. Major Mitchel
had never believed him . . . couldn't trust him
. . . never really forgave him for the booting he
received back at the stage station. A deathbed lie

would stay with a man all the days of his life! He began to laugh.

Then he was gazing down at Hib, whose knees were doubled up to his chest in pain. And as the man convulsed from side to side, twisting on the ground, he kept looking up at Decklin, muttering over and over: "You fool . . . you fool . . . you fool . . ." Decklin's laughter climbed higher in intensity, but it rang empty and hollow.

Aldis was pushing her way through the blocking cavalrymen, trying to get to Decklin, but he was too engrossed with his thoughts to notice her. He began to walk over to where Hib lay, and his laughter ceased as he saw General Sheridan dismount and go to the Confederate's side.

Two troopers sandwiched him between their horses, aiming their bayoneted guns at his chest, the prick of the steel needled sharply into his flesh.

"Back off, Yank," said the corporal, poking the bayonet at his heart. "You already have one foot in the grave; move again and I'll cut the other one off."

Decklin saw the general kneel beside Hib and heard Hib's low, feeble voice mumble, "Lieutenant Decklin lied. He lied, to save me. He was a fool . . . he didn't know then that I killed Colonel Moore . . . I thought the colonel had the gold map . . ." Hib coughed and asked, "Could I see the lieutenant?"

But Lieutenant Walker Decklin was already in the dust beside Hib, taking the Confederate's shoulders gently from the arms of General Sheridan. And there was no longer any fear in the lieutenant that he had once worshiped a man who was unworthy of affection; a kid's faith was paying off and fresh tears stood on Decklin's cheeks.

The general stood, motioned back his men who had crowded in, and said in a low, soft voice, "I never knew Colonel Viking could have a conscience." He shook his head. "It's something hard to believe about that man." He cleared his throat, his admiration for any man with real vinegar in his blood in his voice as he tried to find an easy way out of a tough situation. "Lieutenant Decklin . . . this Confederate has freed you. It will just be a matter of formality to clear your record . . ."

The general was quiet for a moment or so. Only the sound of horses playing with their bit rollers and chains, and stamping restless hoofs, clinked and clamored forth, as men listened to a Confederate colonel's confession.

It was Hib's faltering whisper that penetrated the silence with its pathetic mutter, making men lean forward in their saddles to listen.

"Walk . . ." There was a tenderness in the manner the Confederate said the word. "Walk . . ." he said again, to make sure the lieutenant heard, and he smiled a little at seeing Decklin nod his head. Then Hib Kinsman's right hand was moving up from his bloody midriff to Walker Decklin's face. A smile touched his thin lips as his searching fingers came away wet; and he looked at those fingers with his own blood on them, the blood in turn being washed away with another man's tears. "Be damned, kid," he mumbled, "if you ain't bawlin'."

He looked again to Decklin's face and his smile vanished at seeing the crimson streaks of his fingers dripping down the litutenant's cheeks in two tiny wet trails. He sniffed a little himself and took a deep breath and smiled. " 'Member once you asked me which of my names I wanted carved . . . on . . . my headstone—Kinsman or Viking? We—ll—I agree with you now . . . I've ruined both, so you don't have much choice. Either name don't make much of a man outa me. I'd appreciate it if you'd not use either."

His voice faded; his hands clutched his stomach; the pain was appalling, but with a twisting frown of a grin he thought he had gripped it at last, and could hold it so in those hands, like a wrestler. "I'd like it, though . . . for old time's sake . . . if you'd not bury me in the same ground . . . where I die."

His shoulders gave a shudder and his body twitched, then his head dropped against the lieutenant's chest. After a while, Lieutenant Decklin moved his hand up to the man's face and drew the eyelids closed, letting the crimson of the colonel's gray tunic blend with the dusty blue of a lieutenant's.

Walker Decklin stumbled as he tried to rise with Hib cradled in his arms. General Sheridan saw the pain wash across the lieutenant's face and only noticed then the dark red spot gradually widening on his right shoulder.

Decklin tightened his grip on the man in his arms

and straightened his backbone. And he stood there
facing the general and the mass of cavalrymen . . . he stood there tall and unbending, letting
the tears roll down his cheeks unashamed.

Aldis touched his arm, but he hardly knew she was
there. Julie scrambled among the horses, hurrying
closer to get a better look at Hib. When she did, she
gave a small cry, but her eyes were dry. She turned to
look up at Decklin and said in a firm voice,
"Walk . . . you know what I'm going to do? I'm
going out in the streets and commit an immoral sin,
so I can go down to Hell and marry him."

Decklin looked at her with his cold eyes and calmly
said, "You already did," and turned his back to walk
away, but he stumbled again.

General Sheridan quickly said, "You're wounded,
Lieutenant . . . you're weak. That Confederate
saved you from the firing squad, and I don't blame
you for having a deep liking for the devil . . . but
here, let my men help you, he's too heavy for you to
carry . . ."

Lieutenant Walker Decklin instantly regained his
balance and stiffened his shoulders.

"He's not heavy, sir," the lieutenant said. "He's my
brother." He extended the man's body in his arms a
little toward the general. "I'd like you to meet Hib-
son Decklin."

Then he turned his back on the general and
walked to where the cavalrymen were blocking his
way from the mouth of the canyon. He didn't ask
them to move aside to let him pass; he just looked at

them in the indifference of absolute knowledge that they would, without him telling them. He turned his head to the side and smiled seeing Aldis quickly fall in step with him.

Heading for a large pine at the canyon entrance, his thoughts went to Joel . . . he had a little over two weeks to make it to Texas and start the cattle heading north.

As he laid Hib Decklin down in the shadows of the pine, he was silhouetted against the moon by a patch of night from above, and he knew a man can only live by a lie for just so long. The breath of a man leaves when he tries to tell himself he has no conscience; oh, he can walk and talk, but the man of him is gone.

He was drawing Aldis to him, his arm about her waist, when General Sheridan, standing off at a respectful distance, softly asked, "Lieutenant Decklin . . . you never said where you were from . . . your post? I have to keep the records straight, you know."

Walker Decklin brushed the back of his hand across his eyes, tightened his grasp on Aldis's waist, slightly turned his head and said, *"Fort Hell."* Then, under his breath, he added, *"Fort Destiny."*